ALL'S FAIR

*May you always
find love in your life~*

Julie Coulter Bellon

ALL'S FAIR

a novel

Julie Coulter Bellon

Covenant Communications, Inc.

For Brandon.
Your sweet smile, squishy hugs, and sensitive heart
bring me so much joy. I love you.

Cover image *Ramadan Kareem* by Blight © Stockxpert
Cover image *Military Helicopter Patrols Coast at Sunset* © Wii/istock

Cover design copyrighted 2008 by Covenant Communications, Inc.

Published by Covenant Communications, Inc.
American Fork, Utah

Printed in Canada
First Printing: July 2008

15 14 13 12 11 10 09 08   10 9 8 7 6 5 4 3 2 1

ISBN-13: 978-1-59811-525-3
ISBN-10: 1-59811-525-1

ACKNOWLEDGMENTS

As I carefully researched different aspects of the war being fought in Iraq, I gained a thorough appreciation for the true sacrifice of the military men and women who serve there at high personal cost. Corporal Matthew Blair, a soldier who has served two tours of duty in Iraq as security for military convoys, was especially helpful and gave me invaluable information to add authenticity to the scenes in my story. I can't thank him enough for his time and patience in answering my many questions; please know, Matt, that you have my deepest admiration and thanks for both your service and your time.

I would also like to thank the people who read this manuscript in its various stages and offered great comments, feedback, and encouragement: Marnie Pehrson, Rachel Nunes, Kerry Blair, Meredith Dias, Kathy Leedom, Curt Lowe, Lisa Daniels, Robyn Wood—and a special thank you to Heather Seaton from Boston and Jennifer Felix for helping with my Massachusetts scenes. You guys are amazing. Thank you!

I couldn't do any of this without my family and their incredible support and patience. Brian, Jeffrey, Lauren, Jared, Jayden, Nathan, and Brandon—you are my heart, my life, and my inspiration. I love you.

And last, but not least, thank you to Angela Eschler for believing in the project.

CHAPTER 1

You're a disgrace to this family.

Kristen Shepherd angrily shoved her full wedding skirt away from the stick shift, forcing the car into first gear so she could get some traction on the muddy mountain road. Massachusetts's Berkshire County was known for its incredible beauty, but all Kristen could see was a few soggy feet in front of her. Her father's words were a refrain in her mind, the background cadence to her frustration over the situation she was in. His voice echoed over and over, making her clutch the steering wheel until her knuckles were white. She needed to concentrate on negotiating the small mountain road through the pouring rain, but her thoughts were spinning in every direction. Michael's deception and her father's statement made her feel like the backward teen she'd tried to leave behind so many years ago—the girl who seemed incapable of making good decisions. Why? Why hadn't she seen any of this coming before now?

Pursing her lips, Kristen mentally shook herself. She was a grown woman, not a child. She was a rising star in all the political circles in Washington. She was polished and educated. What her dad thought about her shouldn't matter. *But it did.* That was one of the reasons she'd come back to Boston to be married: a part of her wanted to prove to everyone, including her father, that she'd made something of herself. And instead, it had only confirmed what they'd always said about her. Poor Kristen Shepherd. Such a disappointment to her father. Not like her brother Brandon. Everyone was so proud of Doctor Shepherd serving his country in Iraq. A little sob escaped her throat as she thought of Brandon. She needed him here. He believed in her, and if he were here he'd give her a hug and know exactly what to do. Blinking back the tears, she willed herself not to cry. She wouldn't give her father or Michael the satisfaction. It was embarrassing enough that she'd run away from the church, leaving her fiancé, her father, and all the guests, but she'd needed to get away as quickly as possible. Now she was headed for the one place she'd always felt safe—the cabin.

With darkness fast approaching, she strained to see, willing her tires not to slip in the mud. Wishing desperately for the wipers to go faster, she once again adjusted the ridiculous billows of her skirt away from the stick shift. "Why couldn't I have chosen something plain and simple?" she grumbled.

Her attention momentarily distracted by the volumes of skirt, the car lost traction and began skidding dangerously close to the edge of the road. She cried out as her heart thudded in her chest, but she braked carefully and quickly while trying to maneuver closer to the mountain. She didn't dare look at the ravine below. Just as she regained traction and was moving forward again, the car suddenly stalled. Kristen took a deep breath and closed her eyes. "No, please," she muttered to herself. "You have got to be kidding me." She turned the key again, hoping it would start. After three more tries she was *praying* it would start. The next turn of the key only produced a clicking sound that made her headlights dim each time it clicked. Looking at the white satin pumps she'd spent weeks picking out, she sighed and opened the door. "I can't be more than a mile from the cabin," she said firmly. "I'll just have to walk."

As soon as she stepped from the car, she was drenched. Her upswept hair began falling down, the ringlets now hanging straight and straggly around her face. Her gown was streaked with mud from her first step, and as she hiked the skirt up around her knees, her shoes squished under the gooey muck. She shook her head and looked toward heaven. "Please don't let this day get any worse!" she pleaded as she started up the road.

She now resented the lace and satin she had adored just hours ago, as it did little to protect or warm her body. Shivering uncontrollably, she concentrated on putting one freezing foot in front of the other, willing herself to hurry. The wind and rain whipped through her as she tried to walk along the roadside in the grass. Idly, Kristen wondered if this was punishment for leaving Michael at the altar, but she discarded that thought as soon as it surfaced. After the phone call at the church that had exposed his deception, she'd had no other choice. Briefly closing her eyes, her fiancé's face came unbidden to her mind.

Michael Forbes. The man she had given her heart to and who should have been her husband by now. A bitter smile came to her face when she thought of how easily she'd fallen in love with him. He was a man who was used to getting what he wanted, and she had been intrigued by his air of confidence from the very beginning. He'd traveled the world, he was charming and intelligent, and he understood the craziness of politics that was her daily life—something she'd never found before in dating. They had worked well together. Her stomach clenched into knots at the self-recrimination she now felt at being so thoroughly deceived by him. How could she have been so gullible and trusting? She thought she knew him inside and out, but that had all come crashing down with that one phone call from her bank, just moments before the wedding.

Straightening her back, she pushed down her heartache and concentrated on her anger. She wished she had her laptop with her so she could see the extent of the damage. The fact that he'd tried to transfer funds from her bank accounts to the Al-Rahji bank in Saudi Arabia was bad enough, but Michael was in charge of the finances for all the campaigns the company ran countrywide. Would he have dared to embezzle from Strom and Pierson? In a political consulting agency, image was everything, and they didn't need the scandal. Sighing, she shivered both from the enormity of it all as well as from the cold. Why did Michael even have accounts in Saudi Arabia? Was this really fraud? And if so, was it his first attempt? She doubted it. But she couldn't call the authorities without detailed proof, and she still wanted to ask him what he was doing—and why. He had barely seemed fazed by her accusations. It seemed to have caused only minor tension—his jaw clenching and his brown eyes turning hard and angry, daring her to say another word. He kept saying she would understand everything if she would just let him explain, but she hadn't let him. Something big was going on here, and she was going to find out what it was.

Shaking her head in frustration, Kristen tried again to process what had happened, but she couldn't fathom the depth of his deceit. As she stumbled through the sticky mud in shoes that were not meant for hiking, in a dress that seemed to weigh more and more by the minute, exhaustion began to overtake her. She felt ready to give up her bank account for nothing more than a hot shower and a warm bed. Squinting through the downpour, she thought she saw the log fence that separated their cabin from the neighbor's property. "Thank you," she breathed, her salvation within sight.

Refusing to take one more step on the muddy road, she decided to climb the fence and shortcut through the property, hoping that the trees would give her some shelter from the rain as she walked the rest of the way to the cabin. Hiking up her skirts even farther and gathering the soggy, heavy mess in one hand as best she could, she stepped on the first wooden rung of the fence, steadying herself on the post. She was swinging her leg over when her dress caught. Hearing a terrible rip, she tumbled out of control, landing in a heap on the other side. The tears began to well in her eyes as she lay back in the mud. "Why?" she yelled, pounding her fist into the oozing, watery trap.

Kristen tried to sit up but only seemed to sink farther into the mud. *I wonder how long it would take for someone to find me if I just lie here and die of hypothermia,* she thought to herself. *Would anyone even miss me at this point?* As she was contemplating the ease of such a plan, a low masculine voice shouted over the pounding rain, "Can I help you?"

She looked up at the shadowy form, startled that anyone would be out on this sort of night. Sitting up quickly, she realized how vulnerable she was. Squinting through the darkness, she demanded, "Who are you?"

"I'm Ryan . . ." He stopped. "Kristy, is that you?" He offered his hand to help her up. She looked at the hand for a moment, recognizing the man it belonged to. He still had dark, curly hair, though it was matted to his head with the pouring rain, and his eyes were the same as well. But something was different . . . His face seemed more angular now, she realized, and the dimple in his chin was more pronounced.

Kristen groaned, rolling her eyes toward heaven. *I specifically recall asking You not to let this day get any worse.* "Yes, it's me," she said loudly, ignoring his hand and getting awkwardly to her feet on her own. "What are you doing up here?"

She watched his eyes travel the length of her, annoyed at the surprise she saw. He motioned behind him. "I thought I heard something so I . . ." He stopped. "Where are you headed?"

"I'm going up to my family's cabin for a few days," she said stiffly. "For some *solitude*." He didn't respond, so she added, "My car broke down and I had to walk. I'll just be on my way."

"I don't think so," he said calmly, taking her arm. "You'd better come home with me."

"I will not," Kristen gasped. "Let go of me!" She twisted out of his grasp and began walking toward her cabin. "I don't need your help," she said over her shoulder, just as her pumps got lost in another soggy mud puddle, bringing her splashing to her knees. Ryan was instantly beside her. "Leave me alone!" she shouted, and to her humiliation the tears that had threatened to fall began in earnest.

He took her by the waist and helped her to her feet. "Kristy," he reasoned, "your father hasn't kept food at your cabin for years. The electricity's turned off. If you come with me, you can have a hot bath, some food, and a good night's rest. I've got my sister's kids over for the night; you'll be perfectly safe."

Kristen closed her eyes. She knew she'd be safe with Ryan. In all the time she'd known him, he'd been a perfect gentleman. In fact, it was a sore spot for her. Opening her eyes and looking into his concerned face, she felt temptation flooding her mind. A hot bath did sound much better than a cold sponge bath. But in the same house as Ryan Jameson? That was asking too much. "How do you know my father doesn't keep the electricity on up here?" she asked suspiciously.

He started walking, his arm around her shoulders propelling her to walk with him. "I come up here regularly, and I talk to your father quite often. More often than you, I'd wager," he said, glancing at her meaningfully.

Kristen scowled. She didn't need him analyzing her life. "That's none of your business," she said, pursing her lips.

"Well, it's good to see you haven't lost any of your spunk," he answered with a laugh. "How's your brother?"

"Fine," she ground out, the scowl never leaving her face. This wasn't how she'd pictured the moment she ran into Ryan Jameson again. Of everyone in this town, she'd most wanted him to see what she'd made of herself. Taking a deep breath, she rubbed her shoulders angrily to generate some warmth, but it was no use.

Ryan didn't say anything else, and they trudged along in silence, the lights of his family's cabin growing closer. Kristen didn't think she could walk another step, and the shivering just wouldn't stop. Ryan tried to draw her into the crook of his arm for warmth, but she pulled away.

He let out a snort of frustration before shrugging off his slicker to put it around her shoulders.

"What are you doing out here anyway? Are you running away again?" he murmured close to her ear as he helped her with the slicker, but she was too tired to answer.

Her senses were overloaded and exhausted. She stumbled in the mud, and Ryan caught her. He swung her carefully into his arms and started toward the house. Kristen protested, but he shook his head. "I am not going to let you die of hypothermia because you're too stubborn to see when you need help."

"I'm not stubborn," Kristen argued. "I'm just fine on my own."

"Kristy," Ryan started but stopped as he adjusted her weight in his arms. "I'm not going to argue with you about this. We're almost to the house, and I don't want to have to drag you in unconscious."

Truth be told, Kristen's muscles were shaking and her body didn't seem to be obeying her commands anyway, so she gave up and relaxed. Within moments, he'd carried her into the house and through the living room, grunting slightly before depositing her in front of the bathroom door. "There are fresh towels in the closet. I'll go see if I can find you something else to wear."

Kristen closed the door behind her and tried to undo the row of tiny buttons that stretched all the way down her back. She couldn't do it. Closing her eyes in frustration, she sat on the edge of the tub. There was a rap at the door. "Is everything all right? I don't hear any water running."

There was no way she was going to tell Ryan Jameson the problem. She didn't want his help. But the tub looked so enticing, and she was wet, muddy, and tired. She opened the door a crack. "I can't undo all these buttons to get out of this dress."

It was obvious Ryan was trying to hide a smile. "I'll go get Jennifer," he said. Within moments he was back. "You remember Alex's oldest daughter Jennifer?" he asked. "She just turned six." The girl looked sleepy, but she smiled at Kristen.

"It's nice to meet you, Jennifer," Kristen said, resisting the urge to pull on one of the girl's long pigtails as she'd done so many times to the child's mother. Jennifer looked so much like Alex. It made Kristen miss her old friend—the old days. "The last time I saw a picture of you, you were a little baby! You look a lot like your mother."

Jennifer wrinkled her nose and nodded. "Everyone says that. Uncle Ryan said you need help with your dress."

Kristen turned around so Jennifer could see the buttons. "It's all these little buttons. I can't reach them."

Jennifer rubbed her hands together as if getting ready for the task. "Is this your wedding dress?" When Kristen nodded, Jennifer tilted her head, assessing Kristen's appearance. "You got it all dirty."

"I know," Kristen said. "I'm not planning on using it anymore."

Ryan had been standing at the door listening to the exchange, but at these words he ran his fingers through his hair and abruptly turned, setting the package he was holding on the counter. "I'll go get some hot chocolate going," he said as he walked away.

Jennifer shut the door and stood on a stool to begin undoing the buttons. Stifling a laugh, Kristen watched her in the mirror. The girl was deep in concentration, her tongue sticking out between her teeth. "Do you know my Uncle Ryan?"

Kristen nodded but didn't say anything.

Jennifer continued. "We came up here to help my Uncle Ryan. My mom says he's grouchy because Aunt Victoria's not here anymore," she explained conspiratorially. "So we came to cheer him up because all he does is work, work, work."

"Well, that's nice of you to spend some time with your uncle," Kristen said, hiding her own reaction to the news she'd just heard. Was Ryan divorced? Or had his wife passed away? Why hadn't anyone said anything to her? "Did your Aunt Victoria go to heaven?" she asked carefully.

"No. But my dad said once that she's going to the other place," Jennifer whispered dramatically. "My mom said she's just a lost soul—that Aunt Victoria hurt Uncle Ryan really bad, but it's a hurt that you can't see. That's why we visit him a lot." She jumped down from the stool. "All done," she announced.

"Thank you," Kristen said as she turned around and the fabric gave way. Jennifer's chattiness also reminded her of Alex and all the times she and Kristen had whispered their secrets about their older brothers.

"No problem." Jennifer rubbed her eyes. "Uncle Ryan said you're sleeping in my room. Don't worry about making noise when you come in. My mom says I can sleep through anything." Jennifer opened the door, then asked slowly, "How come you're not getting married?"

Kristen bit her lip, her emotions about her almost-marriage still close to the surface as she contemplated how she wanted to answer the little girl. It was all so complicated. "I just need to think about some things," she finally said, her voice little more than a whisper.

Without skipping a beat, Jennifer informed Kristen, "I'm going to marry Aaron. He's a boy in my class, and when we get married I'm going to have a princess dress and lots of flowers." Kristen smiled. At the sound of Ryan's voice, Jennifer started down the hall, still talking about the Cinderella dress she would have at her wedding. Kristen's smile turned wistful. If only life had stayed as simple as it had seemed when she was six.

She shut the door and locked it. Turning on the water, she stripped away what was left of her ripped and muddy wedding dress. Sliding into the water, she closed her eyes, luxuriating in the warmth. She looked around the bathroom noting there was not a trace of femininity anywhere. No lacy towels, no cute hand soap, no attention to detail. It was stark and clearly stated that Ryan was no longer married. *Why would that matter to me?* she thought, but her emotions betrayed her. Even after all these years, Ryan still evoked feelings in her—feelings she was determined to squelch. Kristen willed herself to think of something else. She sat up and undid some of the pins still in her hair, and the long blonde curls spilled down her back. She lay back down, the simple gesture making her arms ache. She closed her eyes, her mind running through the events of the day—Michael's angry brown eyes watching her walk away, her father's hard, cold stare, and then Ryan.

Kristen sighed, a mental picture of Ryan and his little sister Alex coming to her mind. Kristen and Brandon had spent every moment they could with the Jameson family—until Ryan's twenty-fifth birthday party. That night had changed everything.

Rubbing her eyes as if that would erase her thoughts, she decided she'd feel better after a good night's rest, so she quickly washed her hair and climbed out of the tub. Unfolding the bundle Ryan had left on the counter, she realized they were a woman's pink satin pajamas. *Probably his ex-wife's. Alex would never wear something like this,* she thought. The memories of Alex warmed her. When Kristen had gone away to school, they'd lost touch, and Kristen regretted it. It had been too long. With a sigh, she dried herself off and put on the pajamas. They were a little small on her five-foot-eight frame, but they'd have to do. She draped her ruined dress over the shower curtain rod, mopped up after herself, and peeked out the door. Ryan was nowhere to be seen.

She turned down the hall to the living room Ryan had carried her through earlier. She'd always loved this room, its large stone fireplace the focal point. Smiling, she recalled all the times she and Brandon visited the Jamesons, laughing and roasting marshmallows around that fire. She drew closer to the crackling warmth, hoping it would help dry her hair before bed. That's how she stayed until Ryan came in—her back toward the fire, wrapped in one of the sofa blankets his mother had crocheted.

"I brought you some hot chocolate," he said amiably, his tall frame making her feel small—not something she was used to given the heels she wore at work. "I don't want you collapsing from hypothermia or something."

Kristen smiled wryly, tipping her chin to look up at him. "I think we'd know by now if I had hypothermia." She took the mug from his outstretched hand, noting that his hair was still damp and curling slightly at the back. He'd changed out of his wet clothes and was wearing jeans and a faded Harvard Law School sweatshirt. "Thank you," she said.

He sat down in the overstuffed leather chair across from the fireplace. "So, do you want to tell me why I found you in a mud puddle wearing what I think was a wedding dress?"

"No," she answered quickly, all traces of a smile gone. "I mean, I'm sorry—you've been really nice. I'd just really rather not talk about it," she added, trying to take the harshness out of her voice. Turning to face the fireplace, the image of Michael's angry eyes came back to haunt her.

Ryan got up and stood behind her. "It's okay," he said. "I won't pry. If you do want to talk about it, though, I'm here."

She shrugged and folded her arms, knowing she had no reason to feel defensive but finding the impulse hard to dismiss. "I'm fine, Ryan. Really." *Or I will be once I can sort this thing out.*

"Kristy," he started but sighed when he saw her stiffen. "Why don't you sit down?"

She glanced up at him and, at the sincere concern in his eyes, took a deep breath before sitting down on a large, comfortable loveseat. Ryan didn't say anything. He just took his chair opposite hers again and watched the fire crackle as it died down to embers while he sipped his hot chocolate.

"Do you remember the last time we were up here?" he finally asked softly, still keeping his eyes on the fire.

Kristen closed her eyes for a moment at his words. How could she ever forget it? "Not really," she lied. "It's been a long time. My life has kept me pretty busy."

"I've been following your career," he said. "You've done all right for yourself." Crossing his ankles, he looked at her. "Things really took off for you after you joined Strom and Pierson."

"Yeah, that was a good move," Kristen agreed, a little surprised to hear it from him but secretly glad that he knew something about her career. "Did you know they're the top political consulting agency in the country?" she teased, the old, competitive spirit kicking in like when they were kids.

"What I want to know is how you went from being a campaign writer for an obscure campaign to being interviewed on CNN when your candidate lost the party nomination for president." Ryan gave a little laugh. "I never would have imagined it."

Kristen bristled. "Well, I can't say I'm surprised. Weren't your comments to me a few years ago pretty much along those lines?"

She could have kicked herself. Ducking her head, she took a sip of hot chocolate, wincing and hating the fact she'd let on that she remembered.

Ryan held up one hand and drew his eyebrows together. "No, I don't recall exactly." He paused for a moment, then continued. "Kristy, that night was really confusing for me, and . . ."

"Forget it. I'd rather not talk about it. Besides, it was so long ago that it doesn't matter."

Ryan looked at her as if he wanted to say more, but he didn't. "I thought you did great in your CNN interview. I only caught the last half, but your answers were smart—you knew all the right things to say."

Kristen was glad for the subject change. She was definitely more comfortable with this line of conversation. "That's my job, Ryan," she said, standing. "And I'm good at what I do." She set her mug down on the table beside her.

"You're not the kid I remember," he said, rising to stand next to her. "I thought I knew everything there was to know about Kristen Shepherd."

"It's been years. There are a lot of things about me you don't know, Ryan," Kristen replied, trying to stay nonchalant.

"I've wanted to apologize to you for a long time, Kristy. I hope you know that. But you seemed intent on cutting ties with everyone you knew back here." He slid his finger back and forth around the top of his mug as if he were nervous. "Why haven't you kept in contact with Alex at least? She's missed you, you know."

Ryan spoke softly, but his words were like daggers in her heart. She'd missed Alex as well, but it was just too hard to face the Jameson family. She tried to shake off the memories and focus on the present. She wasn't a shy and backward girl anymore. She was a professional businesswoman who was confident and capable. "I don't know what you mean," she replied, moving toward the hall. "We just grew up and got busy. I still care about her."

He touched her arm, willing her to look at him. "I really am sorry," he said. "I never meant to hurt you."

Kristen's ears burned. "Don't worry about it. I think we're beyond this now." She pushed her fingers through her hair and took a deep breath. "It's been a long day for me. If you don't mind, I'm going to bed."

Ryan nodded his head. "I didn't mean to upset you." He set his mug down next to hers. "Your room is just down the hall. I thought you could sleep in Alex's old room. There are two single beds in there; Jennifer is sleeping in one. Benjamin and I will be in my parents' old room. Do you remember where everything is?"

She nodded her head. "Don't worry, Ryan," she said, starting down the hall. "I can take care of myself." The irony hit her then. Those were almost the exact words she'd said to him when she'd left all those years ago.

CHAPTER 2

The echo from the explosion rattled the walls, causing Captain Brandon Shepherd to grimace and open one eye. Each mortar seemed to be getting closer, and with all the military activity, he knew something big was going on. The insurgents had been active in the last two days, and that had kept everyone busy. As a doctor, it didn't matter whether Brandon was back home in the States or stationed near the Syrian border at a small medical outpost in al-Qaim, Iraq—he was used to long shifts and pushing his body to the limits of physical endurance.

Brandon sat up and rubbed his hand over his face, feeling the stubble. When he'd first come to Iraq, the mortar attacks had kept him awake, but now they had become commonplace, and he'd learned to sleep through them—except for today. Something just seemed different. He'd pulled an all-nighter at the hospital and had only grabbed a few hours of needed rest, but for some reason he felt uneasy and had been unable to sleep. He sighed and pulled his six-foot frame from his cot. If the mortars got any closer, they'd all end up in the bunkers anyway. He dressed in his fatigues, then grabbed his miniature Book of Mormon and slipped it in his shirt pocket before heading for the makeshift hospital. It was silly, but he felt better having the book near him.

Stretching his neck as he walked, he pressed his fingers against his freshly shorn head. Brandon closed his eyes against the sun's rays, which bounced off the metallic walls of the hangar-turned-hospital where he worked every day. The old hangar was said to have once housed Saddam's private jets. No one could really confirm the story, and Brandon found that legends sprang up like wildfire around here, especially if they had to do with Saddam Hussein.

The soldiers had made modifications to the building, of course, by fortifying it and making the operating rooms impenetrable to mortars. Entering the building through a side door, Brandon squirted some disinfectant on his hands and was walking toward the supply closet when Dr. Rachel Fielding walked in, arguing with the doctor beside her. From the volume of their voices, he could tell it was a heated exchange. "Not again," Brandon breathed, heaving a sigh.

"You're wrong," Rachel said loudly, her tone tinged with anger. She barely looked at the doctor beside her as she spoke.

Brandon shook his head. Rachel Fielding was not an easy woman to get to know. She was opinionated and headstrong, but she was also one of the best surgeons he'd ever seen. And one of the most intriguing women he'd ever met. He walked toward the pair, curious as to what the problem was.

"Dr. Winthrop, Dr. Fielding," he greeted them.

Rachel nodded. "Dr. Shepherd. I thought you were off."

"I am, but I could say the same for you. Your shift was over when mine was." He tilted his head toward the two doctors. "Is there a problem? I could hear the two of you from across the room." Brandon looked encouragingly at Tyler Winthrop, who returned his gaze, the frustration evident in his eyes.

"Dr. Fielding and I are having a disagreement on the course of treatment for the little Iraqi boy they brought in this morning. His burns are extensive, and the head trauma caused swelling on the brain. We can't do surgery *until he's stabilized.*" He enunciated the last sentence, looking straight at Rachel.

"He's stable enough, and he should be at the larger hospital in Baghdad," Rachel said firmly. "The medical chopper could get him there quickly, and he would be able to get better medical treatment than what we can offer here. If we wait, he will die." She looked at her watch. "The medevac chopper is doing a dust-off right now; when it gets get back, he should be taken to Baghdad."

"You're getting way too attached to these people," Tyler muttered.

Rachel set her jaw, tucking her hair behind her ear in irritation. "Which 'people' are we talking about, Tyler? We're here to help the sick and wounded, period. And I don't want this little boy to die."

Brandon looked at Rachel, unable to keep the admiration from his glance. Her eyes were on fire with conviction. She was determined to get her way on this.

"Maybe I can help settle this. Who's the doctor on record?" Brandon asked.

"I am," they answered in unison. Brandon smiled. "Who saw him when he first came in?"

"Dr. Fielding did," Tyler admitted. "I came over when I was done with my other patient."

"Rachel, have you looked carefully at all the test results?" Brandon asked. She nodded. "And it's your medical opinion that he can be safely moved?" She nodded again. "Then let's go tell the parents."

Tyler stiffened immediately. "Will you at least hear me out?" he began.

Rachel shook her head and motioned for the interpreter, Nazir, to join them. They started over to the far end of the hangar, Nazir trailing behind as if waiting for Tyler. Brandon looked back and saw that Tyler was still standing where they'd left him, looking a little forlorn. When he saw Brandon watching him, he spun on his heel and walked out. Brandon knew he was angry, but he also knew that Rachel was trusting her gut, and from Brandon's experience it could go either way, and in this instance, he trusted Rachel. They reached the bedside of the little boy, and Rachel immediately went to his side and checked his vitals. Removing the stethoscope from her ears, she took a deep breath and turned to his parents.

"Your son is hurt very badly," she said slowly, then waited for Nazir to repeat her words. "We are only a small medical facility here. He needs to be at a hospital in Baghdad where they can treat his burns and help him wake up. We have a helicopter that can take him there." Nazir dutifully repeated her words, and the parents' eyes widened. The father paced slowly in his soiled dishdasha, a traditional robe-looking garment dragging just above the ground. Finally he stepped forward and spoke in his native tongue. "He wants to know if they can go with their son to the hospital," Nazir said to Rachel.

"Only one of you may go," she said regretfully. "The helicopter will take one of you."

The father spoke to his wife, and she nodded. Turning back to Rachel, he said in halting English, "I will go." She nodded, briefly brushing her hand over the boy's brow, looking at the cuts and bruises that covered one side of his little face, where the shrapnel had made sharp, raking patterns.

"How old is he?" she asked, her voice softer now.

Nazir asked Rachel's question for her and waited for the father's reply. "He is nine," Nazir reported. "His name is Yusuf."

"Yusuf," Rachel repeated. Brandon watched her carefully, having never seen this side of her before. She was always calm, cool, and collected—if sometimes pushy—even in the most dire circumstances. He had seen her fight for respect as a doctor and as a woman while tired beyond words and still treating the wounded. She always seemed to be in control. Yet here, as she watched this little Iraqi boy, she seemed tender and vulnerable. Rachel caught Brandon watching her at that moment, a small blush rising in her cheeks. "I'll make the arrangements," she said abruptly and strode away.

Brandon caught up to her easily. "Hey, are you okay?"

She nodded. "Why wouldn't I be okay? He's going to get the treatment he needs."

"Rachel," he touched her arm. "It's been a long day already. I know you've been working for at least as long as I have. Let me buy you lunch."

"Buy me lunch?" She laughed. "What are you going to buy me? An MRE? Entertain me while we stand in a chow line?"

He stepped away from her. "I got a care package from my sister. But hey, if you're not interested . . ." He left his words hanging, but he knew he had her attention.

"What do you have, Shepherd?" she asked.

"Something I know you'll love," he hinted, raising his eyebrows. He could tell she was trying not to smile.

"I'm not interested in going out with you," she said bluntly, not quite meeting his eyes.

"I didn't ask you to go out with me," Brandon said. "We've both had a hard shift, and I thought you could use some cheering up. I'm willing to share my care package with you, Fielding, but only because I'm being nice."

She lowered her chin. "I'm sorry. I'm not used to men being nice to me without having ulterior motives." She rubbed her shoulders. "Let me get the helicopter on its way, and I'll meet you at the mess tent."

He grinned. "Deal. See you there." He watched her walk away, wondering how a woman could look that good in army fatigues. Taking a deep breath, he turned around and noticed a soldier across the room sitting in a chair holding a bandage to his head. Knowing Rachel would be a little while, he went over to him. "Have you been waiting long?" he asked.

"Yeah, they seem pretty busy," the soldier answered, standing up next to Brandon.

"Let's take a look." Brandon removed the bandage. "You'll probably need some stitches, but it missed the eye." He motioned for the soldier to follow him and proceeded to set up a stitching tray. Numbing the affected area, he deftly began stitching the eyebrow closed. "We're almost done," he said to his patient after a few moments. "That shrapnel barely missed your eye. You're a lucky man."

"Yeah, well my roommate doesn't think so," the soldier said, a small smile playing on his lips. "Last week I hit an improvised explosive device while I was driving *and* was involved in a firefight. He'll hardly come near me anymore in case bad luck is following me around."

Brandon smiled. "Well, I would say just the opposite. Your luck must be pretty good if you've survived all that and come out unscathed. I'd be happy to share a bunker with you."

Brandon put a bandage on the wound and began cleaning up his work area. "I'll see you back here in five days to remove the stitches," he instructed.

The soldier nodded. "Thanks, Doc," he said, and started toward the door. Brandon took a look around. All seemed quiet, which was usually a bad sign. Shrugging off his thoughts, he decided to think about sharing his care package with Rachel. This was a rare chance to see her in a setting other than the hospital.

* * *

Rachel rubbed her eyes, her body beyond tired. She should be sleeping, but she knew she couldn't rest until Yusuf was safely on his way. Even thinking about what had happened to him today made tears burn the back of her eyes. From what his parents had said, he had found an undetonated roadside bomb in a field, picked it up, and when it seemed to be a dud, he'd thrown it behind him, causing it to go off. His life had been changed forever. When he should be thinking about school and friends, he would be fighting to stay alive. Shaking her head, she tried to gather her thoughts as she walked toward the side of the hospital to wait for the chopper. She folded her arms and looked out the doorway. The sun was already high in the sky, but there wasn't much to look at. Unless you were near a river, there wasn't anything green here. It was all orange-brown silty dust that got into everything—clothing, hair, and mouth—and made you long for the moment you'd be able to wash it off.

She thought of Brandon's offer to buy her lunch and smiled. His eyes always seemed to have a light in them, and he had a ready laugh. He was a peacemaker among the medical crew, and she liked his calm demeanor. The fact was, she hadn't had time to think much about any man since her early days in medical school, and her complete focus on her goal of being a good doctor generally put most colleagues off. Brandon didn't seem fazed at all by her businesslike attitude, though. He genuinely seemed to be interested in friendship, and she had to admit she was intrigued by him.

She could hear the rumble of the rotor blades and knew the Black Hawk helicopter was approaching. Since this was generally one of the more dangerous times—landing or taking off—she put on her helmet and ran a hand over her forty-pound flak jacket. *Battle rattle* they called it, because of the sound it made when you moved. Rachel had thought she'd never get used to wearing it while she was working, but she had.

Moving toward the landing site, she waited patiently while the helicopter touched down and the blades stopped turning. "Frank, I've got a little Iraqi boy that needs transport," she told the pilot. He smiled and gave her the thumbs-up sign. "I'll have him ready for you in about fifteen minutes," she promised. She walked back into the hospital and quickened her step. She wanted to find Nazir and tell him the helicopter had arrived so he could tell Yusuf's family. As soon as Yusuf was on his way to Baghdad, she could meet up with Brandon. She liked the thought of getting to know him better.

* * *

Brandon retraced his steps toward his bunk, arriving at a small row of trailers that everyone called *cans*—each one housing two people. He passed by a few tents with soldiers playing cards or writing letters under the flaps. He opened the door to his trailer and looked at his own cot, inviting him to lie down for just a moment, but he knew it would be useless since sleep seemed intent on staying at bay, no matter how badly he needed it. He sighed. A hot shower would feel so good, just to get the sticky sand off his body. The bathrooms and showers were only two hundred feet away, but there was no guarantee he'd get any hot water, and the lines were usually long. He scrapped the idea, not wanting to miss his lunch date with Rachel.

He went to his locker and slid out his care package. His sister Kristen had sent him Kool-Aid, chewing gum, Skittles, and his favorite staples—ramen noodles, Pop Tarts and microwave popcorn. He sent a silent prayer of gratitude, feeling guilty that he hadn't written to Kristen since his transfer to al-Qaim. He just hadn't found the time yet, but he really wanted to tell her how much he appreciated her. Being in Iraq had given him a different perspective on how much his family and friends truly meant to him. Not to mention that the care packages Kristen sent were like a little bit of heaven. The food items—things he had once taken for granted—were a nice change from military food, and Kristen's letters and packages gave him something else to think about besides the broken bodies he was called to fix every day. He grabbed the noodles, popcorn, Skittles, and Kool-Aid before he closed his locker. He'd write that letter tomorrow, he promised himself. Right now, he was going to have lunch with a pretty colleague. Heading back over to the hangar, he decided he'd use the microwave there before meeting Rachel at the mess tent. He smiled at the idea of finally getting to talk to Rachel alone.

He was coming out of the hangar with two steaming cups of noodles when a loud explosion sounded to his right, followed almost immediately by the ear-splitting whine of the proximity alarm. More scattered explosions came from the left until it sounded like they were surrounded. "It's a massive mortar attack," a soldier in front of him shouted, waving his arm for Brandon to get back. "Head for the bunker!"

The entire camp scrambled for cover. Brandon balanced the cups and ran thirty feet to the bunker. More explosions rocked the camp and smoke filled the air. His eyes began to burn as he sat down. Another soldier came in breathing heavily. He slumped down beside Brandon. "Hey, don't you work with that woman doctor?"

Brandon nodded, a feeling of foreboding building within his stomach. "Why?"

"I just saw her running toward the hangar. The colonel was yelling at her to get to the bunker, but she just kept running."

"Rachel," he said softly, blowing out a breath. Carefully cupping the noodles, he headed for the operating room, where he hoped she'd taken cover. Keeping low and running as quickly as possible, he made it to the door of the hospital and burst in, heading straight for the corner where the operating room was located.

Rachel stood when he came through the door. "Brandon," she gasped. She had a small trickle of blood on her cheek. Brandon set the cups on the table and moved to stand beside her.

"What happened?" he asked. "Are you all right?" He immediately used his shirt sleeve to wipe the blood away, trying to get a better look at the wound.

She waved him off. "It's superficial. I was trying to check on Yusuf; we'll have to wait a little longer before the chopper can get him out of here." They both sat down on the floor. "How did you find me?" she asked.

"Somebody saw the colonel yelling for you to get to the bunker. I figured you'd come here." He continued to look at the cut. "You might need a stitch or two."

"You surgeons are all the same. You want to operate on people whether they like it or not." She gave a wan smile. "I'm fine."

He turned, handing a cup of noodles to Rachel before taking one for himself. "I was on my way to meet you for lunch. Now we can have more privacy," he said, keeping his tone light.

She leaned over and her smile grew wider. "You planned this, didn't you?"

Brandon liked it when she smiled; it relaxed her features. "Yes, I planned this mortar attack so we could have lunch together in the operating room. You got me."

Rachel laughed and slurped one of her noodles. "Oh, this is heaven!" Taking a sip of the broth, she leaned her head back against the wall. "You never know how much you miss the simple stuff until moments like this."

Brandon agreed. "There's popcorn and Skittles for dessert," he told her.

Her eyes widened. "You've got Skittles?"

He nodded. "I thought that might get your attention."

She continued eating her noodles. "So, who's sending you these care packages?" she asked.

"My sister Kristen. She's actually getting married today. I had hoped to be there, but they extended my tour another two months." He felt a little pang of regret. "Kristen wanted to wait for me, but I couldn't let her do it. There's no reason she should postpone her happiness on my account."

"Do you know the man she's marrying?"

"I haven't met him, but from her letters, he sounds really great. His name is Michael Forbes. He works at the same political firm Kristen does."

Rachel raised her eyebrows. "Your sister's in politics? What does she do?"

Before Brandon could answer, the alarm sounded the all-clear signal. Brandon stood up. "I wonder what's going on. With all the military operations going on lately, this can't be a coincidence." He walked into the hallway with Rachel following behind him.

They saw Tyler as they rounded the corner of the hospital. "Frank's looking for you," he said. "And that interpreter, Nazir, is waiting to see if you want him to go with you and the Iraqi boy to Baghdad." He turned away without meeting their eyes, and the three of them walked out to the helicopter together. When they arrived, they saw the colonel talking to Frank.

"Colonel Palmer, is everything all right?" Tyler asked, saluting him.

"They're getting more creative." The colonel grimaced. "They put mortar tubes into some buckets of water, froze them, then put them all around the perimeter. When the sun melted the water, the mortars dropped, hit the bottom of the metal buckets, and fired. That's why it seemed we were surrounded."

Tyler shook his head. "Who thinks of these sort of things?"

"Something big is going on. And I'm willing to bet it's about the summit later this week. Having the leaders of Syria, Iran, Iraq, Britain, and the U.S. in the country is just too tempting for the opposition, so they're trying to distract us with stuff like this." He looked over at Frank. "We're tightening security at the Syrian border, but there's a group of insurgents in al-Qaim that ambushed our guys a block north of the main square. We've got an urgent and a priority that need evacuation," the colonel said.

"We're headed over there now," Frank said. "One of you docs want to come with me for the urgent patient?"

They heard several explosions behind them—probably more melting mortars, Brandon thought—but he and Rachel instinctively ducked.

"I'll go," Rachel said, coming up behind the men.

"No," Brandon and Tyler said simultaneously.

"There's no time to argue." The colonel took Rachel by the arm. "We need to be up in the air now." Rachel turned back to talk to Nazir, who was waiting near the entrance to the hospital. "The Iraqi boy will have to wait, Nazir. We've got some priority patients near the main square in al-Qaim. Will you wait?"

He nodded and, without saying a word, headed back into the hospital. "Your Cobra escort is waiting," the colonel told Rachel, propelling her to the door of the helicopter.

"I'm coming with you," Brandon said, patting his own flak jacket and adjusting his helmet. "If that's all right with you, Colonel," he amended. "Dr. Fielding may need my help with two patients. The insurgents are obviously close by, and they don't seem to care we're medical."

Rachel and the colonel nodded, and they all climbed aboard the helicopter with Frank, a soldier, and the crew chief. Rachel briefly looked back at the base, then at Brandon. For a millisecond he thought he saw fear in her eyes, but it flickered and was gone.

"Be careful," Tyler said as the helicopter rotors started turning, then he crouched down and headed back toward the hospital.

The crew chief fingered his M-16, watching the landscape carefully for snipers or rocket-propelled grenades. Brandon kept his own eyes peeled, watching the scenery as it went by, finally turning his attention to the blue-gray sky which was a strange color that looked warped because of the heat waves rising from the earth. They passed over a shepherd with his sheep, and Brandon thought that if he didn't know better, he would never have believed this was a war zone. When the Black Hawk was at treetop level, Frank started darting and zigzagging, trying to be a difficult target. A downed American helicopter, even one with a red cross adorning its bulbous nose, would be a major coup for the Iraqi insurgency. Brandon rubbed his eyes and glanced over at Rachel. She was struggling to open the large medical supply cases that had been stashed at their feet. He helped her, and they looked through them together. Everything seemed to be in order, but Rachel picked up each instrument and bandage, handling it, and mumbling to herself. "What are you doing?" Brandon asked.

She didn't answer right away, and he just watched her, at the same time pulling the Skittles out of his pocket and opening the package. Only then did she glance over at him. "I'm familiarizing myself with the location of everything so that when we're in the middle of an emergency situation, I won't have to go looking for something." She eyed his Skittles. "You know, we never finished our lunch."

He chewed slowly, looking at her. "You're *familiarizing* yourself with the location of everything?" he asked.

She slapped him on the shoulder. "Yes, now can I have some Skittles or not?"

He poured some into her hand. "You're cute when you're impatient." Before he could say more, the helicopter jolted, slowed, and started its descent. "We've only got a few minutes," Frank shouted back at them. "There's a sandstorm coming, and the Cobra team is waving us off. If we go, though, those men will be on their own, and

I don't want to leave them behind. Load and go, that's what we want, so let's get a move on."

Rachel and Brandon quickly surveyed the scene. A Humvee, still smoking, lay on its side, blown up by an improvised explosive device—the weapon of choice for the Iraqi insurgency. Some small-arms fire could be heard in the distance. Three U.S. soldiers were trying to form a protective perimeter around the downed Humvee, and the Cobra was providing some assistance, keeping the insurgents at bay. Rachel and Brandon quickly hopped out, each grabbing a medical case, the soldier who'd come with them following closely behind. Brandon looked up as he saw the sky darkening, unable to believe his eyes. A large, menacing black cloud of dust, dirt, and debris was barreling toward them. "Hurry!" Frank shouted. "The sandstorm's almost here!"

As they started moving forward, the Cobra pilot swooped in and picked up Frank's crew chief so the wounded would fit in the helicopter with both doctors. Then the helicopter circled back to pick up the three U.S. soldiers who were providing ground cover. The Cobra pilot shouted, "I'll cover you from the air, but get out of here, Frank, there's nothing more you can do. Go now! That sandstorm's right on top of us, and I don't want to come back here looking for you!"

Frank nodded and waved the Cobra team off. "You go. We're fine—don't worry about us," he called back.

Rachel nodded at Frank's gesture to hurry as she reached the wounded soldier on the far side of the perimeter. Brandon headed for the wounded man nearest the burning Humvee. The man was pinned beneath the vehicle, his legs obviously crushed. "I need some help over here," Brandon called to the soldier they'd come with, but he was already helping Rachel get her patient situated and moving toward the helicopter. "We've got to get the Humvee off him," Brandon yelled to Frank.

Frank started to unbuckle himself from his pilot's seat. "I'm coming," he shouted. Brandon nodded and felt for vitals on his patient. The soldier's pulse was weak. Time was of the essence.

At that moment, Brandon heard a strange whine, and it seemed as if everything went into slow motion. Frank climbed out of the helicopter and took two steps toward Brandon's position just as a rocket-propelled grenade hit the tail rotor of the Black Hawk. The helicopter exploded, throwing everyone backward. Brandon slammed into the ground just as the dark sandstorm cloud descended on them, making everything coal black. Brandon's ears were ringing, and his shoulder felt like it was on fire. Smoke filled the area, mixing with the sandstorm and making it almost impossible to breathe. Brandon found some semblance of cover from what was left of the Humvee and tried to take deep breaths. The side of Brandon's head was wet and sticky, and he knew he had a head wound. In the force of the blast, his helmet must have come off. He felt around as best he could, searching through the blinding sand until he found the soldier he'd been working on. Reaching for the man's wrist, he tried to find a pulse and realized the soldier was dead.

Brandon felt torn between venturing farther out into the storm to find Rachel and the others and staying put. He began coughing uncontrollably, the sand whirling around him as though the devil himself were stirring it up. He lay still for a moment, trying to assess his injuries and taking shallow breaths. When he was finally able to sit up, he felt disoriented, and a blinding pain in his head caused him to wince. Brandon tried to get his bearings, determining he had to try to find the others. He crawled on his hands and knees, digging through the sand and going in the direction he thought the helicopter had been in, remembering that Rachel had been trying to move the wounded soldier. He moved slowly, reaching out like a blind man with a cane.

"Rachel," he called, his voice scratchy with sand. He thought he heard a faint cry and moved toward it. A few feet ahead, he felt a human hand, and as he scraped through the dirt and sand, he realized it was the soldier who'd been helping Rachel. He was lying at a grotesque angle, obviously dead. Brandon's stomach sank. "Please let Rachel be all right," he murmured to himself. His eyes were watering, and he could barely see the inches in front of him as he frantically searched for her. Within a few minutes, he heard a voice, "Brandon?"

"Rachel, I'm here!" he called. He crawled toward the sound of her voice. Finally reaching her, he grabbed her arms, trying to pull her toward him. She was lying on her back, and he could barely make out a trail of blood slowly seeping from a wound on her forehead. "Are you all right?" he shouted as he gently shook her shoulder. She squinted, trying to open her eyes, but she didn't answer him, so he leaned closer. "Are you hurt?" he asked again over the roar of the storm.

She sat up slowly, shaking her head. Her voice was raspy. "My head hurts, but I think I'm okay." She rotated her shoulders and turned her head. "We've got to get out of here. I can barely breathe."

They both scrambled backward to where the Humvee was, their only sure source of cover, and ducked under it as best they could. Brandon was grateful that at least the sandstorm had suffocated the fire that had been burning on the vehicle, but he hoped it wouldn't suffocate them as well. Time seemed to stand still, and Brandon couldn't gauge how long they'd been huddled near the vehicle. After what seemed like hours, the sandstorm had finally spent its fury. Rachel and Brandon huddled together, pulling the collars of their uniforms up over their faces and doing their best to breathe as they lay partially buried in the sand next to the Humvee. Brandon tried to shield Rachel as much as he could, but the tiny, scratchy sand particles caked every surface they landed on. He could smell the burnt rubber and hear the crackle and hiss of the fire from the helicopter, but he could only see the sand in front of him. And Rachel. He decided to concentrate on her.

"Are you still all right?" he asked as he began to dig them out of the massive sand pile they were sitting in.

"I think so," she said slowly, helping him dig.

He suddenly held up his hand. "Do you hear that?" Brandon felt the ground shaking beneath him, then he heard the low rumble of trucks. But he wasn't alarmed until he heard guns being shot into the air and men shouting. Brandon's heart began to pound as the blood in his veins seemed to turn to ice. He looked into Rachel's eyes and knew that she had come to the same conclusion he had. They began looking for weapons, trying to stay low while attempting to wrench open the burned-out door to the Humvee. But it was to no avail. Everything was buried in sand and debris. They were trapped.

They crouched lower, watching three trucks approach. When the small convoy reached them, several masked men got out and surrounded the downed helicopter. They located Frank and the soldier Brandon had found, digging out their bodies and turning them over, talking to each other in loud voices as they worked. Brandon peeked around the body of the Humvee, and, at that moment, a man who appeared to be the commander looked up and met Brandon's eyes. The man stared for a moment, his expression cold. He stroked his short beard, his expression calculating as his eyes bored into Brandon's. He began pointing and speaking to his men, his voice low.

"Make a run for it, Rachel," Brandon urged quietly. "He's seen us!"

"I'm not leaving you," she whispered fiercely. "Besides, there's nowhere to run."

Brandon silently agreed, and they looked at each other for a long moment, knowing these seconds could be their last. He grabbed her hand and squeezed before they both stood, wiping the sand from their faces. They were soon surrounded by men wildly gesturing with their AK-47 machine guns.

They took Brandon first, hustling him away from Rachel and forcing him into the back of one of the trucks. He craned his neck to look back at Rachel and briefly saw her wide, frightened eyes. He felt a flash of pain as the butt of a rifle connected with his head. And everything went dark.

CHAPTER 3

When Brandon came to, he opened one eye and came face-to-face with a pistol. He sat up slowly, as the man with the gun watched him closely, making sure the weapon followed his every move. Brandon raised his hands and met the man's eyes, their deep brown depths showing nothing. He winced as he tried to adjust his position while he continued to stare at the end of the gun that could end his life at any moment. His head throbbed with the most intense migraine he'd ever had. Pushing himself toward the edge of the truck, he tried to get closer to the wheel well, where there seemed to be a little more space. The flapping canvas canopy was the only covering over the long truck bed he lay in.

Brandon took in his surroundings, noting the wooden boxes wedged in between Rachel, himself, and two armed guards. From the looks of it, Brandon guessed the guards were about his age; they were wearing fatigues and keffiyehs in the turban style. The man sitting near Rachel had his face partially covered, the only thing visible being his small eyes, which darted back and forth between the two captives. Their guns were at the ready as the truck bounced along, hitting every pothole in the dirt road. *At least Rachel and I are together and alive,* Brandon thought to himself. He licked his lips, the heat of the day settling over him and adding to his frustration. He looked at Rachel, who was sitting across from him. She still had a small trickle of blood on her cheek, and the wound on her forehead looked angry and red, but other than that she looked fine. "Hey, Rachel. Are you okay?"

She glanced up at the guard before replying, and when she turned her eyes toward Brandon, he could see her fear. "Do you think the soldier I was working on before the helicopter exploded survived?" she asked.

Brandon thought of Frank and the other soldier. Both had obviously been dead. He slowly shook his head.

"Shut up," the guard sitting next to Rachel growled. He kicked his foot toward her. "No more talking."

Brandon clenched his fists. He knew that even if there had been any survivors, their captors probably would have either killed anyone who was still alive or taken them hostage with him and Rachel. He closed his eyes, feeling helpless and wishing he were anywhere but here. From the look on Rachel's face, she felt the same. "Are you sure you're okay?" he asked again.

The guard put the gun next to Rachel's head. "No more talking or I will make sure she never talks again, okay?" His accent was heavy, and some of the words were hard to make out, but his meaning was very clear.

Brandon held up his hands. "Okay. No more talking." He watched Rachel; her eyes were panicked, but she gave him a barely perceptible nod. She was okay.

The guard next to Brandon started speaking to his counterpart in a language Brandon didn't understand. Whatever he said seemed to mollify the other guard, and everyone relaxed a little. Rachel caught Brandon's eye as she put her elbows on her knees and subtly pointed to her head. Brandon gave a ghost of a smile. She was obviously trying to ask him about his head. He nodded to tell her he was okay. It hurt, but it was probably just a mild concussion. Not something he'd die from.

At his nod, Rachel turned away; then, quick as lightning, she turned back and moved her body closer to the guard who seemed the most reasonable and calm. "We're doctors," she said forcefully, looking straight into his face. "Doctors. We help people." He stared at her, not saying a word. "Doctors," she said again, her voice dropping to a whisper. Glancing at the cab of the truck, she folded her arms across her chest. "Where are you taking us?" she demanded.

The guard sighed. "You will learn silence," was all he said.

Brandon's entire body felt tense; he couldn't believe Rachel had risked such an outburst in the face of armed gunmen. Surprisingly, however, the guard hadn't seemed especially perturbed. Brandon leaned forward and put his head in his hands. The pounding in his head was reaching a fevered pitch, and his throat was scratchy. What he wouldn't have given for a drink. He touched his shirt pocket, which he couldn't actually feel through his flak jacket. Knowing his Book of Mormon was still there somehow made him feel better.

Rachel made a move as if to sit next to Brandon, but the guard next to her stopped her with the foot of his boot. "Move again and I'll have to kill you," he said as if he were discussing the weather. Brandon watched the man's finger twitch on the trigger and motioned for Rachel to get back. The guy meant business, and the guard sitting next to Rachel made no move to intervene this time. Rachel obeyed and returned to her previous position.

The truck began to slow, and they could hear wild cheering and gunshots that got louder as they approached. Brandon peeked out the small opening between the canopy and the truck, and his stomach sank. Black smoke wound in a column into the blue-gray sky as people gathered around several burning trucks as if they were campfires. The truck stopped, and the guard urged them out of the back with the barrel of his rifle. More guards met them as they climbed out—the men from the other trucks in their convoy. Brandon felt sick as he looked at the scene before him. Men were everywhere, cheering at the charred remains of several U.S. military vehicles.

"The rebellion has begun." The guard who had threatened Rachel sneered in her face. "Soon you will see what we are capable of."

"No!" Rachel screamed as she stepped forward, having caught sight of what the men were cheering over. A guard grabbed her around the waist, but she pushed him away. He pulled her closer against him, laughing as she struggled.

Brandon lunged for the guard. "Get your hands off her!" he demanded. Before he could intervene, however, another guard stepped in, muttering something to the man who held Rachel. He nodded and released her, but from the leering look in the man's eyes, Brandon knew it wasn't over.

"Stay here or you will be killed. No one here looks kindly on American soldiers," the man said to Rachel, loudly enough for Brandon to hear.

They stood rooted to the ground, somewhat sheltered near the back of the truck as they watched the macabre celebration. The air was filled with the sounds of shots being fired and the cheering of the men. Rachel hugged herself, tears brimming in her eyes. "Do you think there are any wounded inside those trucks?"

Brandon glanced at the smoking remains of the trucks. "We can't help them if there are, Rachel. We'd be killed ourselves."

The guards, who had been listening to the conversation, shook their heads and laughed. Pointing their guns in the air, they fired off several shots, joining in the apparent jubilation, making Brandon's head ache worse. He looked closely at the burning vehicles but didn't actually see any signs of human life. *Maybe they got out before they were hit,* he thought hopefully. *If not . . .* His heart ached at the thought of their fate. Clenching his fists, he turned to Rachel. "I'm so sorry."

She turned tear-filled eyes toward him, then glared at her captors. "Why?" she shouted. "Have you no compassion at all?" The guards laughed again, and one grabbed her by the arm to drag her back to the truck. Brandon followed, a rifle at his back. Before they could be hustled into the truck, however, Brandon caught a glimpse of a familiar face. Rachel spotted it, too. "Nazir, what are you doing here?" Rachel gasped. Nazir took a quick look at them, then disappeared into the crowd. "What's going on, Nazir? Help us! Tell them who we are!" Rachel shouted at his retreating back.

Nazir's head bobbed through the crowd before it was swallowed up in the mass of people. Brandon and Rachel were herded back into the truck, but Brandon's focus remained on Nazir and what his presence potentially meant. Had this been a setup from the beginning? His thoughts were quickly brought back to the present, however, when he saw that the seemingly more level-headed guard was not getting into the truck; only the leering guard had climbed aboard. Brandon was instantly on alert. The guard shoved him to the very front of the truck, telling him to go behind a wooden box and stay there. He forced Rachel to remain near the entrance with him. Rachel curled up, hugging her knees and crying softly. Brandon crouched near the edge of a box, watching Rachel carefully, wanting nothing more than to comfort her. The truck lurched away, and Brandon fought down nausea as his head began to pound. The pain was almost too much to bear. He wondered if it might be better if he just passed out. Yet leaving Rachel alone with this man was not an option.

* * *

Rachel's head ached as much from exhaustion as from the wound on her forehead. She lay her head on her knees and tried to clear her mind. The rocking of the truck almost lulled her to sleep. Almost. The guard sat so close to her she could smell his body odor. She curled up as tightly as she could, trying to block out the memories of the helicopter, of Frank, and of the soldier she had been trying to treat before the sandstorm. It all seemed like some horrible nightmare she could not wake up from.

She stole a glance behind her and saw Brandon watching her. She was intensely grateful for his presence. It was comforting to know someone cared about her. It had been a long time since she'd had that. Shortly after her parents had moved to Dallas, when Rachel was in high school, they had been killed in a car accident. She'd been sent to live with her grandmother. It had been a relatively happy, although sometimes lonely, existence until her grandmother had been diagnosed with cancer. Then it became one long round of taking her grandmother to chemotherapy and radiation treatments. However, it was this that had first sparked her fascination with the medical field. She soon knew all the doctors and nurses on a first-name basis and grilled them for information. They had become her mentors and had helped her become what she was today, a successful doctor. Her grandmother would have been proud of her. She produced a mental picture of her grandmother and thought of how many times she'd told Rachel that she'd always be there for her. Rachel brushed away an unbidden tear and wished she were with her grandmother now. "Help me out of this," she whispered to herself.

* * *

For the first hour, Rachel sat motionless on the floor, her head on her knees. Brandon watched her and the guard carefully, occasionally looking out beneath the flapping canopy to see the scenery passing before them. It was barren, with occasional bits of sagebrush and few landmarks. He thought they might be on the road to Fallujah, though the silty sand that was kicked up by the truck in front of them made it hard to discern much of anything. Several scenarios ran through Brandon's mind as they traveled, but he couldn't make sense of them. Where did Nazir fit into this? Was their kidnapping connected to what was happening with the military buildup around the city of al-Qaim, where they'd been stationed, or was it just a crime of opportunity? Were both of the insurgent attacks today part of something bigger?

Out of the corner of his eye, Brandon saw the guard suddenly move closer to Rachel. The hairs on Brandon's neck stood up. The man had his back to Brandon as he sat behind her, scooting as close as he could. Putting down his gun, he reached for Rachel's arms, pulling them gently away from her knees. Rachel whimpered, "No." The guard paid no heed and quickly forced her to the floor of the truck, his sheer size dwarfing her smaller body. As Rachel screamed Brandon's name, he shot forward, quickly grabbing for the gun while the guard's attention was distracted, reaching it a split second before the guard likewise reached for his weapon.

"Let her go," Brandon commanded, putting the barrel of the gun to the man's temple.

The guard seemed surprised but didn't release Rachel. Instead he trailed his finger down her cheek. Brandon shoved the barrel of the rifle hard against the back of the guard's head. "I said, let her go." His voice was barely more than a growl.

The man got up slowly, raising his hands toward Brandon as Rachel crawled away as quickly as she could. At that moment the truck slowed, and Brandon looked out. They were rolling to a stop in front of a large two-story home. "Let's make a run for it, Rachel," he said softly, still pointing the gun at the guard. He knew it was risky, but it was the only chance they had. Rachel nodded. "Now!" Brandon said.

They jumped out the back of the truck, rolling on impact. Brandon grabbed for Rachel's hand, and they took off down the road. He glanced back to see the guard banging on the cab of the truck and felt his stomach clench. They didn't have much time. Although he felt disoriented from the pain in his head and didn't know exactly where they were, he focused on simply getting away. It looked like they had stopped in a village, since houses surrounded them, but the homes appeared abandoned. Brandon pulled Rachel toward him and they ducked into an alley. He put the strap of the rifle around his neck and quickly peeked around the corner. Several men from the convoy of trucks were fanning out, shouting to each other as they went.

"Over here," he said to Rachel as he ducked beneath an empty clothesline.

She nodded, her breath coming in gasps. "I've never been so scared," she said, her voice shaking. He squeezed her hand, and they ran between two houses, crouching down to listen. Brandon tried to take stock of their surroundings. His eyes came to rest on an old car parked across the way. He pointed across the street. "Do you see that car?"

"It looks dead." Rachel shook her head.

"It's our only choice," he said. "We've got to try." He glanced around the corner. "No one's coming. Let's go."

He stood and ran, with Rachel right behind him. Hearing shouts, he jumped into the car and ducked down. Rachel ran around the other side and got in, quickly sinking to the floor. Brandon started pulling wires from below the steering column and, after finding the right combination, began twitching them together.

"What are you doing?" Rachel asked, glancing behind her.

"I'm trying to hot-wire the car," he said, his breath coming fast.

"Where did you learn to hot-wire a car?" she asked, incredulity on her face.

Before he could answer, the glass of the passenger-side window shattered. Rachel screamed and instinctively covered her head. Brandon flicked the wires once more. The car remained lifeless. He picked up the gun and opened his door, trying to pull Rachel out on his side, but they were surrounded before he could even get out of the car. The man in front of them held out his hand for the gun. Brandon held onto it for a moment, debating whether they could shoot their way out.

Suddenly a round went off near their feet, startling Brandon by its closeness. The decision was made. He handed over the weapon and put his hands up. Rachel did the same. Brandon hung his head in defeat. With gun barrels pressed against their backs, they began the long walk back the way they had come.

This time the guards weren't taking any chances. Brandon and Rachel were both blindfolded, their hands and feet tied tightly. Brandon's blindfold was slightly skewed, however, so that he was able to see out of one side. He saw that they were being dragged into the large home the truck had stopped in front of earlier. They were then pulled down a small flight of stairs and thrown into a room in the basement. Brandon heard Rachel moan softly, and he scooted closer to her. "Are you all right?"

"I'm okay," she assured him. "But these ropes are cutting off my circulation."

"Can you sit up?" He moved next to the wall and propped himself up. Rachel did the same. Mercifully, their hands were tied mercifully in front of them. Brandon eyeballed the knots and began to pull at them with his teeth. "Maybe we can loosen them a little."

She shook her head. "It hurts worse with every move I make."

"We have to try, Rachel, or we'll suffer more later on. Please."

They worked on their bindings for several minutes until they heard footsteps approaching. The door opened, and Brandon tried to peek under his blindfold, but he was hauled unceremoniously to his feet before he saw much.

"Come," a guard growled.

"Where are we going?" Brandon asked. "What do you want with us?"

The guard slapped him on the side of the head. "Shut up and maybe you'll live."

Brandon heard Rachel call his name, and he struggled to turn toward her, but the guard's grip was like a vise around his arm as Brandon was dragged forward. He felt himself pushed through a small doorway and roughly thrust into a chair before his blindfold was removed. He squinted his eyes, trying to adjust to the light, and realized he was in a small room, sitting in a chair facing a table that had a video camera on it. "Hold this," the guard commanded, shoving a newspaper into his still-tied hands.

Brandon awkwardly took it, his mind racing. He had seen video footage of kidnapping victims when he'd been back in the States, and it usually hadn't ended happily. He knew he could very well be taking his last breaths. "What do you want? Do you want money?"

"We want to show your government that you are a coward and a traitor," the guard said, adjusting the camera.

"I am a doctor," Brandon said. "Under the Geneva Convention, you have to allow me safe passage."

The guard sneered. "You are here to take our country and our oil. The Geneva Convention does not apply here."

At that moment the door opened, and a man dressed in army fatigues entered. He was tall, had an angular face, and a small beard that traced along his jawline. Brandon recognized him as the man who had first spotted him and Rachel near the Humvee. He strode toward Brandon, leaning in so close they almost touched noses. They eyed each other for a moment, then he straightened. "Bring in the woman."

Brandon lifted his chin. "Leave her out of this," he said, his voice urgent. "Tell me what you want."

"I think you will be quiet and do as you are told," the man stated. "I am Mofak Jassem. You are now a prisoner of war."

CHAPTER 4

Kristen awoke to the sounds of people at the breakfast table. She stretched, feeling warm and comfortable in the bed. Then the events of the day before came crashing back around her—Michael's face when she'd confronted him, her mad dash from the church, and ending up in Ryan's house. Groaning, she turned over in bed, then got up as the sound of children's voices filled her ears.

Opening the door, she ran her fingers through her hair and padded down the hall to the kitchen. Ryan's sister Alex was sitting at the kitchen table, examining the dark rings under her brother's eyes. "What happened to you?" Alex asked him, arching a brow.

Ryan only grunted. Kristen stood near the doorway; no one had noticed her yet. "Well, I have some interesting news," Alex said, watching Ryan closely. "Do you remember Kristen Shepherd?" Kristen cringed. "Well, out of the blue I got a wedding invitation, so I thought it would be fun to see her after all these years. I went to her wedding yesterday, but before I could even say congratulations, she left her fiancé at the altar."

Kristen put her hands to her cheeks, feeling the burn of embarrassment. The children, who had been eating cold cereal at the breakfast bar, stopped when they heard their mother's conspiratorial tone of voice and leaned forward as if they wanted to hear better. Ryan didn't reply, and his back was to Kristen so she couldn't see his face.

"Don't you think that's odd?" Alex pressed. "I mean, I've hardly heard from her in years, and I was so excited to go to her wedding and see her. She deserves to be happy after all she's been through. And now this. It's so sad."

Ryan ran his hands through his hair. "I don't think it's any of our business," he murmured.

"Hmm . . . So what's eating at you this morning?" she asked, touching his arm, sisterly concern filling her voice.

Ryan let out a deep sigh and, sounding a little exasperated with her, said, "Nothing, Alex. I'm just tired, that's all. I didn't sleep well last night."

"Did the kids keep you up?" Alex asked doggedly as she reached out and poured herself a cup of orange juice.

"No. It's not that." He turned toward the children. "Hey, Ben, did you tell your mom you are now the family Chutes and Ladders champion?" His obvious attempt to change the subject made Kristen smile. She breathed a sigh of relief and hoped Alex would go along with it.

"It's true," Benjamin announced smugly.

Kristen watched as Alex gave her brother a small smile before she went over to stand by her son and ruffle his hair. Kristen knew exactly what Ryan was doing to their conversation. *Some things never change,* she thought with amusement. "Congratulations, buddy," Alex said to Benjamin. Moving toward her daughter and giving her a hug, she asked, "How come you look so tired this morning?"

"Uncle Ryan had to wake me up to help his friend undo her wedding dress. It was such a beautiful dress, Mom, but she ruined it with the mud all over it." Jennifer turned back to her cereal and didn't see her mother's quick look at Ryan.

Alex raised her eyebrows. "What's your friend's name, big brother?" she asked.

Kristen had been busy watching the family drama unfold before her and hadn't realized that Ryan had turned and was watching her. Alex's eyes followed Ryan's, and Kristen stepped into the room, pushing back her hair. "Hey Alex," she said, trying to act nonchalant. "These two munchkins definitely have your genes. They have a voice that can carry for miles, just like their mother's."

Alex laughed and went over to hug her friend. "Hi, yourself," she said. "What are you doing here?"

Kristen's eyes darted to Ryan's, but he didn't meet her gaze, so she went ahead and sat down at the table. "Your brother found me rain-soaked down by the property line and probably saved me from hypothermia by forcing me to come here."

Alex sat down next to her. "My brother saves a damsel in distress, then bosses her around?" she mocked, shaking her head. "Tell me what happened yesterday. I was so surprised to get your wedding invitation. How have you been? I've really missed you, you know."

Ryan looked up at Kristen. She felt at a loss for words with all the questions Alex had just fired. He shook his head slightly, then jumped in before she could say anything, his expression unreadable. "She needed some solitude and was trying to climb the fence near her old cabin in the pouring rain and fell. I found her lying in the mud, shouting at the sky."

Alex laughed and touched Kristen's arm. "That sounds like you. I think I passed your car on the road coming up here. I'm guessing Ryan told you that your dad doesn't even keep electricity up at his place anymore."

"Yeah, I told her, but I'm not sure she believed me," Ryan said as he stood, pushing his chair back from the table. "Someone should probably call your dad and tell him where you are so he doesn't worry."

"I'll do that," Kristen said quietly, not meeting his eyes. "When I'm ready."

Ryan drained his cup of hot chocolate and paused in the doorway. "I better go and see if I can get someone to tow Kristy's car to town."

Alex nodded at her brother, then turned back to Kristen. "I'm sorry about what happened yesterday at the church, you know. But I'm even sorrier it's been so long since we've talked."

"I know. I'm sorry about that too," Kristen said with a smile. "Just listening to you talk tells me you haven't changed a bit. And I've really missed that." Looking down, she grimaced. "Tell me honestly, how bad did it look yesterday?"

"It wasn't horrible. Just a lot of people speculating, that's all. Your dad is probably pretty worried about you." She glanced at Ryan, who was still watching them from the doorway. "It's also in the news this morning since Michael is from such an influential family." She gave her friend a sympathetic look. "Do you want to talk about it?"

Kristen closed her eyes. "I was hoping the media would respect our privacy, but I was obviously wrong. I can't believe anyone would be interested in anything we do, but you're right, the Forbes family is legendary in Massachusetts." She looked from Ryan to Alex, then down at her pajamas. "I should get dressed." She moved to get up, then sat back down. "I guess I don't have any clothes."

Alex started to rise, but Ryan held up his hand. "I scrounged around and found some sweats and a T-shirt of Alex's. I set them on the bathroom counter for you."

Kristen didn't meet Ryan's eyes but thanked him and got up from the table. She hesitated for a moment, then squeezed by him as she turned toward the bathroom.

Alex's eyes followed her down the hall. It seemed like she wanted to say something but she just smiled at Kristen as she sat down to watch TV with the children. Kristen could tell Alex had a million questions, but she assumed that after the years apart, Alex probably didn't feel as comfortable demanding the dirt as she had in their teenage years.

Kristen shut the bathroom door, grateful for a little time alone to gather her thoughts. She changed her clothes and did the best she could with her long hair. Looking into the mirror, she wished she had some makeup to help her look a little less pale. She pinched her cheeks and shrugged her shoulders. It was the best she could do. Walking back into the kitchen, she grabbed a piece of toast, still debating on whether or not she should call her dad. Deciding she needed a bit more time, she walked toward Mr. Jameson's office. It felt good to be back in this house, somewhere familiar and safe. Ryan's dad had always been so good to her. As she approached the door, she could hear Ryan's deep voice making arrangements for Kristen's car to be towed to town.

She knocked and hesitantly entered the room. Ryan was straightening some papers. "Come in and make yourself comfortable," he invited, motioning to the chair in front of what was now probably his desk.

Sitting down, Kristen looked around. "I don't think I've ever been in your father's office. He was usually out in the family room playing games with everyone."

Ryan followed her gaze. "I loved sitting in here late at night, just talking to him. He always had time for me." He stopped and Kristen could tell by the look on his face that he regretted the words, probably remembering how Kristen's father never had time for her. She wanted to reassure him that she'd come to terms with it, but after yesterday she wasn't sure about that anymore, so she remained quiet. He looked away without finishing his thought. "When I'm up at the cabin, this office is really convenient for taking care of any business that comes up in town."

"Brandon told me about your dad passing away last year," Kristen said. "I was sorry to hear about it. He was a good man." Her gaze lingered on him for a moment, but then she broke the eye contact and abruptly changed the subject. "I hear you have some good news, though. You were chosen as the governor's new chief of staff? Somehow I never imagined you in politics."

He smiled. "I enjoy it, surprisingly. I love being an attorney, but being the chief of staff brings something new and different every day. I was surprised by the appointment, but I really believe in what the governor's trying to accomplish, and I like to think I'm helping him meet his goals."

"You'd make a good spin doctor," she said, meeting his eyes. "From what I've heard, the governor isn't doing very well by the people of Massachusetts; he's just another Washington puppet."

"That's not true," Ryan disagreed. "Cameron Mitchell has done more for education in this state than any previous governor, *and* he's been able to balance our budget. He has only the people's interests at heart."

"He hasn't compromised at all? Are you sure about that?" Kristen challenged.

Ryan took a deep breath. "I don't think I want to get into a political debate with you, Kristy. I watched you on CNN. I know how good you are." She felt a slight blush creep up her neck, and it irked her a little that he could still pull such a reaction from her.

She recovered quickly and asked, "So, I just wanted to know what was happening with my car. Is it repairable?" She met his eyes, lifting her chin slightly.

"I don't know. I have a towing company on their way to pick it up. You know I'm not very mechanically inclined." He chuckled, hoping to draw a smile from her, but she merely stared at a point beyond his head.

"I suppose I should try to catch a ride back into town." She sighed and sank down in her seat, covering her face with her hands. "I was really hoping to stay away for a while, but I can't stay up here with no transportation."

Ryan came around the desk so quickly it startled her. He leaned against the edge and folded his arms. "Kristy, you're welcome to stay up here as long as you want. You know that."

She lifted her face to look at him, feeling vulnerable. Everything seemed so familiar and so different at the same time that it was confusing. "You're the only person who's ever called me Kristy," she murmured. He didn't reply, and they stared at each other for a moment. Kristen wondered if he was thinking back to that night long ago that had changed everything between them. The tension in the air was palpable. She opened her mouth to say something, but at that moment, Alex walked in.

"Kristen, if you'd like . . ." When she saw the two of them, her eyes widened and she backed up. "I'm sorry if I'm interrupting something."

Ryan dropped his eyes and straightened. "I was just telling Kristy she's welcome to stay here if she likes."

Alex nodded her head. "There's no better place to get some perspective, you know."

Kristen shook her head. "You're both very kind, but I would never dream of imposing."

"You've never been an imposition," Ryan said softly.

Kristen stood, almost knocking the top of her head into his chin, feeling a desperate need to get out of there before any more old emotions resurfaced. "Thanks, but I don't think so. Alex, do you think I could get a ride into town?"

"Sure," Alex said, drawing her brows together in confusion at Kristen's sudden impulse to leave. "I'll go gather the children's things."

Kristen moved to follow her, but Ryan grabbed her arm. "Kristy, I'd like to talk to you."

Kristen looked down at his hand on her arm before gently breaking free. "There's nothing to talk about, Ryan. I'm not a lovesick girl anymore, and you don't have to worry about me."

"It's about Brandon, actually."

Idiot! Why did I have to say that? She groaned inwardly. *Stop acting like a teenager,* she scolded herself. Taking a deep breath, she asked, "What about Brandon?"

"When was the last time you heard from him?"

"A couple of weeks ago, why?"

"Just wondering, that's all. He hasn't answered any of my letters or e-mails for a while," Ryan explained.

"I've written several myself that he hasn't answered, and I sent a care package to him. I thought for sure he'd write and tell me he got it. Do you think we should be worried?" Kristen drew her brows together in concern.

"Hmm. Well, you've heard from him more recently than I have. So I guess we shouldn't worry. He's probably just busy. His last letter to me said he was moving near al-Qaim. Maybe our letters haven't reached him yet; that's a pretty remote area. You know the mail system out there."

"You're probably right," she agreed.

"I'm really interested to see how the Security Summit in Baghdad turns out," Ryan added. "Hopefully we'll get some idea of when this war will be over and when Brandon will be home permanently."

"That's what I'm hoping for, too," she said. Walking toward the door, she turned. "And thanks again for helping me last night." She watched him, and for a brief moment she saw an air of maturity and sadness that she'd never seen before. It made Ryan seem vulnerable; the Ryan she knew had always seemed strong and untouchable. Resisting the urge to admit he probably wasn't the same man she'd left behind—and that they'd both changed—she merely nodded her head at his "You're welcome" and closed the door. If there was one thing she'd learned, it was to never underestimate people and to never show weakness. And she wasn't about to start now.

CHAPTER 5

Rachel was brought into the room and pushed into a chair next to Brandon's. She swallowed, and it looked like she was trying hard to remain calm. The guard began to untie her hands and feet. Mofak Jassem, who was talking to the cameraman, sauntered over to her. He took her by the arms, pulling her to her feet to give her a thorough once-over. Rachel shivered, and Brandon knew she must be terrified. He had to give her credit, though; she raised her chin and faced the man before her. "What do you want?" she asked.

"Do not speak to me," Mofak growled. "You will learn your place." He shoved her to the far end of the room.

Brandon strained at his bonds. "Leave her alone!"

Mofak ignored Brandon and pushed Rachel against the wall. He began undoing her flak jacket. "No!" Rachel said loudly, pushing at his hands.

He slapped her face hard. "Shut up," he hissed through his teeth. He practically tore the flak jacket from her, and she stood before him in her fatigues. She tried to run, but he grabbed her and threw her back against the wall. He snapped his fingers, and one of the guards held her in place while the other brought forth a large piece of black material.

Rachel struggled, her voice coming in gasps. "You'll have to kill me first," she ground out.

Mofak acted like she had not spoken. "You will be appropriately dressed when you are in my presence and before we take you to see Sayed," he informed her. "Put this on."

Brandon felt weak with relief. They only wanted her to wear an abayah. They also had a head covering for her. Rachel closed her eyes for a moment, then quickly put on the long, black garment and the head covering. When she was finished, she was escorted over to sit next to Brandon. Grabbing his hand as best she could, Rachel gave Brandon a tremulous smile.

Mofak covered his head and part of his face with a keffiyeh and began to speak. From the rhetoric, Brandon knew the cameras must be rolling. Mofak held the gun close to Brandon's head as he talked about the war crimes of the United States and the slaughter of innocent civilians near al-Qaim. Then he turned to Brandon and Rachel. He prodded Brandon. "State your name."

"Brandon Shepherd. I'm a doctor at the field hospital in al-Qaim and a captain in the United States Army." Brandon shifted in his chair, and the guard standing behind him pushed him forward.

Mofak raised Brandon's chin with the end of the gun. "Why are you here?" he demanded.

"I'm here to help those that are wounded and sick," Brandon answered.

"Those who are wounded and sickened by the actions of your government," Mofak sneered. "You are part of a great conspiracy to take our land and all of her resources. You kill innocent people only for financial gain." He walked over to stand next to Rachel. "Do you know what has happened to the women in our country? To the men? The dignity and respect of our people have been taken away because of the actions of your government. Don't you see?"

Rachel was silent. Mofak squatted down beside her, putting the gun near her face, running its cold steel down her jawline. "Do you have the same answer as your colleague? Are you here to help those that are wounded and sick?"

Rachel tried to turn her face away. "Yes."

"We will see." Mofak turned to look directly into the camera. "We will prove to the world that the Americans are cowards who will do anything to save their own lives—even become traitors to their own country." With that, the camera was shut off, and Mofak removed the cloth from his face. "Take them back to their room while we get ready," he ordered.

Brandon sucked in a breath. That didn't sound good. Several images of what they could have planned for him and Rachel went through his head. In that moment, he made up his mind that he would behave honorably—no matter what happened.

The guards took Rachel out of the room first, half dragging her down the hallway. After Brandon's feet were untied, he was escorted close behind. Brandon watched Rachel walk woodenly through the door, obviously trying hard not to trip on the material from the abayah. They were both thrown into the empty room, the door locked securely behind them.

Rachel hurried over to him and untied his hands. He rubbed his wrists, trying to restore the circulation and relieve the prickling sensation. He looked into Rachel's face, seeing the naked fear in her eyes. "We're going to get out of this," he said, trying to sound reassuring.

She shook her head. "And how do you see that happening?"

Brandon sighed. "I don't know yet. I'm sure we'll think of something."

"How do you think they're planning to make us betray our country?" she asked, her brown eyes full of apprehension. "My imagination is running pretty wild right now."

"I don't know." At his answer, she turned away from him, and he saw her shoulders begin to shake. "Rachel?" Brandon asked quietly. Her tears surprised him, but he went to her and gently turned her around to face him. "It's okay. I'm here," he murmured as he gathered her in his arms. "Shh . . ." he whispered into her hair.

"I'm sorry. I haven't slept in almost twenty-four hours. I can't even think clearly." She looked up at him and wiped her tears away. "I'm glad you're here."

"Me too." Brandon felt the dizziness return, but not wanting to alarm Rachel, he simply smiled encouragingly. Pulling her toward him, he sat down against the wall and drew the half-eaten bag of Skittles out of his pocket. "Didn't you say we hadn't had time to finish our lunch?"

She gave him a smile. "You know, Skittles are my favorite. Are you sure you want to eat them now? Who knows when they're going to feed us."

He offered her a handful. "You're right; we should ration what we have left. But I think it's worth a few Skittles right now if it helps get us through this."

She took the candy from his hand. "Thank you," she said. She chewed silently for a moment, closing her eyes. "If you were home right now, what would you be doing?"

"I'd probably be at the hospital," he said with a smile. "I don't seem to have much of a life beyond medicine."

She smiled back at him. "Me either." She gathered the abayah material close around her feet. "What do you think they're going to do with that videotape they took of us?"

"Probably broadcast it somewhere. That's the good news, I think. Then everyone will know we've been captured, and they can start a search-and-rescue mission," Brandon replied.

"Do you really think they will?" Rachel asked.

"Of course. They can't do without us." Brandon chuckled. "I mean, without us, there's only Tyler left. They're definitely going to want to rescue us."

Rachel smiled. "You've got a point there." She turned to study Brandon with a concerned gaze. "Hey, are you okay? You look really white."

Brandon tried to nod, but he could feel the blackness at the edge of his consciousness pressing in. "I'm going to pass out, Rachel. I'm really sorry."

She leaned forward. "Don't leave me alone here, Brandon, please."

He fought for consciousness but could only squeeze her hand.

CHAPTER 6

Kristen walked into her childhood home, jaw set, ready to face her father. But he wasn't home. *Just as well,* she thought, going into the dining room to pour herself a glass of milk. The newspaper was on the table, a picture of Michael and herself staring back at her from the front page. "Forbes Wedding Called Off," the headline said. She groaned and scanned the story. It talked about Michael's career, his family, her own career, and how they'd met at the PR firm. And how, at the last minute, Michael had addressed the crowd, saying that there had been a delay and that there wouldn't be a marriage that day. The bride was nowhere to be found and speculation ran rampant as to where she had gone and why. Kristen closed her eyes. If that phone call hadn't come when it did, she would have married Michael and maybe never even been the wiser once their names and accounts had been joined.

She threw the paper back on the table and went up to her room to pack her things. It was strange to be in this house. She had her own upscale apartment near Washington, D.C., but this place still felt like home to her. Entering the room she'd spent her teenage years in, she saw that everything was practically as she'd left it, right down to her mirrored dresser, the ribbon she'd won from debate club in high school hanging from it. Sighing, she looked at her reflection in the glass. Dressed in Alex's old sweats and T-shirt, she looked eighteen again. Running her fingers through her hair, she sat down on the edge of the bed and opened the top dresser drawer. Pulling out a picture, she traced the four smiling faces looking back at her. Brandon and Ryan stood close together, pulling her and Alex into the picture. They were all laughing, and at that moment, Kristen wished she could go back to those days. Fingering the engagement ring in her pocket, she knew it could never be so.

Standing, she took the ring out of her pocket and set it on the dresser. Pulling her suitcase from the closet where she'd placed it the week before, she started packing. Just then, her cell phone rang, jarring her from her thoughts.

"Kristen Shepherd," she said into the phone, using her most professional tone.

"Kristen, it's Jack." Instantly, a picture of Jack Pierson entered her thoughts. Jack was a dynamo, a legend in the political world. If you wanted someone elected, you hired Jack Pierson's team. He was thorough, detailed, and a dangerous opponent, but Kristen loved working for him. He had been an incredible mentor to her, teaching her the tricks of the trade, and his energy was contagious.

"What can I do for you, Jack?" she asked, a smile on her lips. "I'm supposed to be on my honeymoon, you know."

"Supposed to be?" He immediately latched on to that important phrase. "I thought I heard something about that on the news this morning. There are a lot of people speculating. So it's true, then?"

Kristen sat back down. "I just couldn't go through with it." Kristen was silent for a moment, debating whether to ask the question on her lips. Finally she said, "Jack, you've known Michael for a lot of years. Did you meet him before or after he came back from working in Saudi Arabia?"

"After. I liked the fact that he had international experience as a diplomatic aide, although he's hardly ever talked about it. Why?"

Kristen thought back to the phone call from her bank and bit her lip. Something wasn't right. She'd thought she knew Michael so well, but obviously she had somehow missed part of the puzzle—and she was going to figure out what it was.

"No reason. I was just wondering. Did you ever meet his ex-wife, Madj?"

"Ah, well, that explains it," he said carefully.

"Explains what?" Kristen kept her tone neutral, not wanting to give anything away.

"No. I've never met her, but I know he keeps in contact with her. The divorce seems to be amicable from what I can gather. I think she's in Riyadh now, though."

He keeps in contact with her? Kristen's thoughts ran wild. *When? How?* Taking a deep breath and briefly closing her eyes, she calmed her racing thoughts. She needed to look into this further, but not now—and not with Jack.

"You're not jealous, are you?" Jack's voice pulled her back from her thoughts.

She sighed and changed the phone to her other ear, not wanting to admit what she suspected was really going on but knowing she needed to. "Jack, it's not jealousy. I'm trying to figure a few things out."

"Like what?" he pressed.

Kristen bit her lip. "Have you ever had any problems with Michael's work?"

"No. Is there something I should know about?"

Taking a deep breath, Kristen plunged on. "I got a call from a bank in Saudi Arabia right before the wedding saying that Michael had tried to empty my bank accounts. I'm wondering if he's been skimming off company books as well, since he's apparently willing to fleece his own fiancée." She sighed and added softly, almost to herself, "Love without trust never lasts." Kristen sat down on her bed, feeling the tears start to gather. The sense of betrayal came rushing back to her as she remembered her confrontation with Michael the day before.

Jack's voice was steady, but she could hear a hint of surprise in it. "There must be an explanation for this. Did you try to talk to him?"

"Yes, I did, briefly at the church. He was upset but said he would explain after we were married. Obviously that didn't happen. He's left several messages on my cell phone, but I haven't returned them."

Jack tapped the phone. "Michael has seemed nervous and edgy this past little while, but I chalked it up to wedding jitters. I don't know what's gong on here, but one lesson I've learned in this business is that there are two sides to every story, and you need to remember that," Jack admonished. "I'll start a quiet internal investigation since he has had access to all of our funds, and I'll have any transactions he makes closely monitored. I can't believe he would steal from the company, though."

His tone was thoughtful. "That said, I'm glad you told me about this, and I'm glad you followed your instincts. I always knew you were listening to me when I told you to trust your instincts." Kristen could hear papers shuffling in the background as Jack continued. "I'm sorry, kid. I thought you and Michael would make a great team, but marriage is a tough thing under the best of circumstances. I tried it twice myself." He chuckled, and his tone was softer now.

Kristen knew she couldn't take any sympathy today. "Thanks. Listen, what can I do for you?" she said.

"I've got an amazing job offer for you; I knew you'd want to know about this right away." Jack was back to business. "Xavier Addison is running for governor in Massachusetts against Cameron Mitchell, but he's not getting results. He's been campaigning all over the state, and he isn't satisfied. He wants our team to finish his campaign with a win."

Kristen took in a breath. Xavier Addison was well known, and with his wealth and government experience, he'd be a formidable candidate. "That's great, Jack. You know I can do it."

"I know. That's why I'm calling. And this will be opportune, in light of the information you just gave me. Since I thought you'd be married, I put you and Michael on the team together. Perhaps, if you're comfortable, you can help me monitor him until this situation is resolved. What do you think? Don't feel obligated if it's a problem."

That's going to be a big problem, her brain cried out. "No, no problem at all," she heard herself say. "We're both professionals, and I want to see this ironed out as much as you do."

"Are you sure, Kristen? I need you to be focused. This situation is a tough one, even for you." His tone was almost fatherly, and Kristen felt determined not to let him down.

"It's fine," she reassured him. "I will be focused. Don't worry." Kristen paused and debated asking the next question. But she had to know. "Jack, let me know what your investigation turns up, okay?"

"I will. "When she didn't say anything more, Jack continued. "Good, then it sounds like we're set. Since you're available now, I'll tell Addison we can go ahead and announce the addition of our team on Monday. Ready for his contact numbers?"

Kristen reached into her bag for her notebook and copied down all the information. "Okay, boss, I've got it."

"Xavier's got his eye on the White House, so this campaign could be really important for your career," Jack said.

"Every campaign is important to my career, Jack. I'm building my record," she said. "Don't worry—Addison's a candidate I can work with."

"Keep me informed, even on the details," Jack said before hanging up. Kristen touched the END button on her phone and looked at the numbers she had written in her notebook. She'd just accepted a job heading up the campaign for the next Massachusetts governor. A thrill went through her at the thought of a campaign, but it was quickly squelched by the idea of being near Michael, as well as the thought of going up against the current governor—and his chief of staff, Ryan Jameson.

She heard the door slam downstairs and knew her father was home. Taking a deep breath, she went downstairs. He was still in the doorway, taking off his jacket. Kristen folded her arms. "Hello, Dad."

"There you are," he said, glancing at her. "Why didn't you call? I've been worried."

Kristen was surprised at his words. *He was worried?* "I went up to the cabin to think about being a disgrace to the family."

He stared at her for a moment. "Kristen, I'm sorry I'm so blunt sometimes, but your decisions aren't always ones I agree with. You know that. I thought we had an understanding." Shrugging his shoulders, he changed the subject as if everything were resolved. "I don't have electricity up at the cabin anymore. I'm surprised you would even go there." He looked at her a moment. "We haven't used that thing in years." He walked toward her and stood in front of her, giving her a once-over. Kristen resisted the urge to stand up straight. "I should have known that's where you would go. I know you and Brandon have some great memories there. Are you all right?"

His tone was soft, and in that moment, Kristen could actually believe he cared about her. She hadn't felt this way for so long she didn't know how to react. "I'm fine," she said automatically. "Ryan Jameson was up at his place with his family, and he helped me out."

"Did you tell him you had run away again?" He chuckled, and it made Kristen angry. What would he know about it?

"No, I didn't. But I'm sure he guessed what had happened when he found me practically frozen to death in a wedding gown," she said coldly.

He didn't respond but patted her shoulder and moved toward the kitchen. "Ryan Jameson. Now there's a good man. So are you going to tell me what this is all about? Why did you leave the church like that?"

Kristen sighed. "Actually, it's a long story, and I've got a lot to sort out."

"Well, maybe we can keep it a little more private next time." Kristen felt the embarrassment rush to her face again, so she turned away to look out the kitchen window.

"That young man was pretty upset over the way you left him. He stomped out of the church muttering that he needed to fix this right away. He seemed pretty anxious."

I'll bet, Kristen thought. *Especially if he was counting on fleecing me out of all my money.* Why transfer it to Saudi Arabia though? It just didn't make sense. Why would Michael do something like that? "Well, I accepted a job this morning, so I'll be sticking around Boston for a while, if that's okay with you."

"Fine with me." Her father grabbed an apple out of the bowl on the table, retrieved a paring knife from the drawer, then pulled out a chair and sat down to peel his apple. Kristen turned and watched him for a moment. It was a ritual Kristen had seen him perform every morning up to the day she'd left home. "You can have your old room back if you want," he said.

Kristen nodded and, feeling like she'd been dismissed, turned and went upstairs. She felt like a little girl again. *This is temporary. I am a different person now,* she told herself. Squaring her shoulders, she knew she would have to prove it.

* * *

Kristen stood at the podium on a makeshift stage. She was looking out over Boston Commons and preparing to introduce her candidate. It was invigorating to be standing there, a slight wind in her face, feeling in control. The last twenty-four hours had been crazy. She had made a few discreet calls to contacts she had, trying to see if there had been any whispers of financial problems for Michael—or any other reason why he would want to steal from her—but so far she'd come up empty. She couldn't understand why he'd done it. He wasn't necessarily wealthy, but he wasn't poor either. There was no reason for it that she could see. But her personal investigation would have to take a backseat for the moment because she was busy laying the groundwork for her transition onto Xavier Addison's campaign team. She wanted her team to hit the ground running.

This press conference was crucial, and she had personally overseen every detail. The only drawback was Michael standing directly behind her. He put his hand on her shoulder, and it was all Kristen could do to resist the urge to shake it off. He knew she would never make a scene in public, especially in front of a press corps, and it irked her. She couldn't wait to confront him, to make him answer her questions, but she would bide her time until she felt prepared—physically, mentally, and emotionally. She considered that maybe it would be a little easier if she approached it like a job.

Pulling back from her thoughts, she focused on the crowd before her, pointing her hand toward the historic marker that indicated where the British army had stationed themselves as they'd occupied Boston. Her amplified voice boomed over the microphone, and she felt the surge of adrenaline. This was the perfect placc to kick off their leg of the campaign against the current governor. She wanted the public to look at Governor Mitchell as the occupying force, consumed by his own policies. And she wanted them see her candidate as the leader who could take them to eventual victory and a better life for everyone. The symbolism of their location was just too perfect. Moments like these rejuvenated her, and she let the excitement flow over into her voice. The crowd cheered, and the reporters inched ever closer with their microphones as she finished her introduction and the candidate strode to join her at the podium.

Kristen stepped back, and Michael leaned over to whisper in her ear. "Well done."

She nodded, and he continued as they walked back to their seats. "We need to talk, Kristen. Let me explain."

Kristen smiled as she sat down, but the smile didn't reach her eyes. "I know we do. But not here, not now."

"I want you to understand, Kristen. Anything I've done, I've done for us."

"Are you kidding me?" Kristen shot back incredulously, turning to look at him. Several reporters on the front row turned toward her, and she composed herself again, smiling and facing the crowd. "We'll talk about this later," she said as she leaned forward. "You can bet on it." Michael only nodded.

After two hours of glad-handing the right people after the press conference, Kristen was finally able to go home. She sank into the chair nearest the door, slipping off her pumps and stretching her feet. It had been a long and satisfying day overall. The kickoff to Addison's campaign had gone off without a hitch, and the campaign team seemed especially sharp—except for Michael. That had been the only blight to the day. She'd tried to give her engagement ring back to him, but he wouldn't accept it, telling her he'd win back her trust and love. Not likely at this point. His declarations of love fell flat. *Love without trust never lasts*, she told herself again. They had been a good team once, but she doubted they ever would be again. She had told him that she would be contacting him within the next day or so to hash things out. Part of her dreaded the confrontation, but mostly she just wanted to get it over with. Sighing, she closed her eyes. Her phone rang, interrupting her thoughts, and she reached over to answer it.

"Kristen Shepherd," she said crisply.

"Kristy, it's Ryan." His deep voice was warm and calm, and her breath caught in her throat at the familiar sound of it.

"Ryan. Are you back in town?" she asked, trying to sound only mildly interested.

"Yes, I had to come back to work today. I caught you on Channel 5 this afternoon. Looks like you'll be sticking around for a while."

"What I wouldn't give to have been a fly on the wall when the governor saw that press conference," Kristen admitted with a little laugh. "Will you tell me what he said?"

"No, but I'd like to talk to you. Can you meet me for dinner? I'll bet anything you haven't eaten yet, and you probably skipped lunch."

Kristen's first impulse was to decline. But she was hungry, and the frozen dinner in the freezer didn't sound as good as eating out with Ryan. "Okay. Where do you want to go?"

"Well, if I remember correctly, you love stuffed quahogs, and the best place for those is Legal Sea Foods. What do you say we go to the one across from the aquarium?" He gave her the address, and she agreed to meet him there in half an hour. It was a little unnerving that he remembered things like that about her. It had been years since she'd had the stuffed clams. But the reality was that the four friends had spent a lot of time together. It just seemed so long ago now.

She pulled into the parking lot of Legal Sea Foods and took one last look at herself in the mirror. Telling herself she didn't care what Ryan thought of her now, she betrayed herself by applying a little lip gloss. She got out and smoothed her blouse, knowing the dark blue set off her blonde hair. As she entered the restaurant, Ryan waved to her from a far table.

"You found it," he said as he stood to greet her. He was still in his suit, but his tie was slightly askew; she knew his day had probably been as busy as hers.

She sat down. "It wasn't hard. It's like riding a bike, I guess. Thanks for inviting me." The waitress handed her a menu, and she opened it. "What can I do for you, Ryan?" Kristen asked.

"I wanted to talk about your new job. Do you know what you're getting yourself into?" he asked, getting right to the point.

She closed her menu just as the waitress reappeared. "I'll have your stuffed quahogs with the New England Clam Chowder and a salad, please." She decided she might as well indulge her love of clams while she was here. There wasn't any place in the world that made them better.

The waitress nodded. "I'm Heather, by the way. Can I get you anything to drink?"

"A sparkling water with a lemon twist and no ice, please, Heather," Kristen replied. The woman took down her instructions and left. "Yes, Ryan, I know what I'm getting myself into. As you may be aware, I've run a few campaigns before. And won."

Ryan scowled. "I know. What I want to know is why you took *this* job? Why stay in Massachusetts now?"

"I have my reasons," she said, her voice cool.

"Aren't you working with your ex-fiancé?" he asked.

"Ryan, what are you getting at? Why do you care what I do or who I work with? We haven't seen each other in a really long time. We're not close. What makes you think—" Before she could finish her sentence, a camera flash went off in her eyes, momentarily blinding her.

"What was that?" Ryan asked, blinking.

Before either of them could react, a reporter was standing in front of them and a few more flashes went off.

"Mr. Jameson, as the governor's chief of staff, why are you meeting with the campaign head of Mr. Addison's new team? Is the governor worried about the race? Are you discussing strategies?" The questions were rapid-fire, and Ryan started to get up.

"No comment," he said as he motioned for Kristen to follow him. She pushed her chair back and slid out from behind the table to stand beside him.

"Ms. Shepherd, do you have anything to say?" the reporter asked, grabbing a pen and small pad of paper out of his pocket.

"What's your name?" she asked pleasantly.

"It's Todd Prentiss." He reached to shake her hand. "Are you going to tell me why you're meeting with the governor's chief of staff? Does Mr. Jameson have anything to do with the reason you called off your wedding?"

"Not at all. We're old friends, and he offered to buy me dinner, so I accepted," she said. "There's nothing more to it."

The waitress chose that moment to bring out Kristen's soup and salad. "If you'll excuse me Todd, I've had a very busy day, and I'm hungry." She sat back down and motioned for Ryan to do the same.

The reporter nodded and was about to walk away when he turned back. "Here's my card. Feel free to call me if you ever want to talk." He took one last look at them, his smile unmistakable as he gave Kristen an appreciative once-over.

Kristen returned his smile and thanked him, then turned back to Ryan. "Where were we?"

"Kristy," Ryan's expression was incredulous. "What are you doing? You're not going to call that guy, are you?"

Kristen rolled her neck. "Ryan, this business is all about contacts. I just made a new one."

"He wants to be more than a contact," Ryan muttered.

Kristen dug into her clam chowder with gusto, and Ryan seemed content to do the same. When they were finished, Ryan leaned forward. "Have you talked to your dad?"

"Of course. He offered me my old room back." She searched his face for any reaction to that, but Ryan's face was inscrutable.

"I hope you can work things out with your dad. He's just a lonely man who doesn't know any other way besides the military one. That's why he is like he is."

"Ryan, I don't expect you to understand. Your father was warm and loving, always interested in what you were doing. If my father is lonely, it's because he's driven away everyone who ever loved him." Kristen put down her fork. "Did you really call me here to talk about my father?"

"No, I wanted to clear the air between us. I wanted to apologize—"

Kristen didn't let him finish. "There's nothing to apologize for, Ryan. You said what you said; I said what I said. I thought there was more to our relationship than there was, that's all. I thought I loved you, but you loved Victoria, and that's that. Obviously, I wish you hadn't said those things about me to Victoria, but they were probably true, and it motivated me to get out of Boston and start living my own life," she finished, mustering a smile. "Let's just forget about it."

Ryan sat back. "Kristy, I did something I thought I would never do when I told Victoria those things about you, and I wish you hadn't overheard us. I never wanted to betray your trust. She knew that we were close, and she was a little jealous, so I was just assuring her that I didn't think of you that way."

"You told her about my mother's death, how it had made me dependent on everyone around me because of my shyness and insecurity. You said I was so closed off I would probably live my life taking care of my father, trying to win his love, and end up lonely and alone."

Ryan cringed. "You remember it that clearly?" He tilted his head and looked at her closely. "I'm so sorry. I don't even know what to say."

"It hurt me to hear you say I was closed off; you and Alex were the two people who knew the real me. At least I thought you did."

She fiddled with her napkin. "When I confronted you I wasn't closed off. When I told you I was in love with you . . ." She searched for the right words. "You didn't laugh," she finished lamely. Kristen took a sip of her water, trying to collect herself. She'd replayed that conversation in her head for years.

"Ryan, it hurt me at the time, but like I said, it was the best thing that could have happened to me. I realized I probably *was* closed off and had limited myself to our safe little foursome. My feelings for you were limited—you were someone safe, but you didn't feel the same way about me as I did about you. When we had our little conversation that night, I realized I had been living in a fantasy world, and it jerked me into the real world. So I should thank you. Since then I've experienced life and love like I should have, and I'm glad about that."

"You've experienced life and love, huh?" Ryan said. "Anything you'd like to share about the life lessons you've learned? Or why you had to completely cut off contact with Alex and me to learn it?"

Kristen bit her lip and carefully worded her response. "You and Alex were good to me when I needed a friend. I'll always remember that, Ryan. We had some good memories, and that's all. I needed to get away, to prove myself." She looked at him, at his curly dark hair that had been tamed carefully with gel. His green eyes bore into hers, and she knew he thought she was dodging his first question.

"Is that all it was?" His look silently asked her for the truth, entreating her to tell him something, but she knew she couldn't express it now. Maybe not ever. "What were you trying to prove, Kristy?"

She needed to change the subject fast; her stomach did flip-flops as he narrowed his eyes, probing hers. "We should grab Alex and her family and go out to dinner, all of us. I'd like to get to know her again." Kristen made her voice bright—a little too bright. "I still can't believe she married Dave Meyers right after I left. I always thought she wanted to go to law school first, like you."

Ryan leaned back and put his napkin on the table, but Kristen could tell from his body language that the subject wasn't closed yet, although he seemed willing to let her change the topic. "I guess Dave swept her off her feet," he said, chuckling. "Those two were so right for each other. I thought she got married too young, but it's worked out for both of them." He leaned forward, his elbows on the table and his face so close to hers she could smell his aftershave—still the same spicy, outdoor scent that was uniquely Ryan. "What about you, Kristy? Why didn't you get married?" he asked, his voice low.

Smooth, she thought. *Right back to where we started.* Putting on her game face, she debated with herself. Part of her wanted to tell him the whole story—to go back to the way things had been between them for so many years. Brandon, her usual confidant, wasn't here, and it would feel so good to pour out her heart to someone, to tell them her suspicions about Michael and how hurt she was. But she didn't know Ryan anymore—not enough to trust him like that while her heart was still wounded. "I could ask you the same question," she shot back, softening her remarks with a winsome smile. "What happened to your marriage?"

He looked uncomfortable. "It's a long story."

"I thought so." She gathered her purse to leave, feeling a little more confidence build in her after seeing his reaction. "I guess we'll be in two separate political camps for the next six weeks." Standing, she looked at him. "You know what they say: All's fair . . ."

"In love and war," he finished for her. "Is that what this is going to be, Kristy? A war?"

She smiled and raised her eyebrows before turning on her heel and letting him watch her walk away.

CHAPTER 7

The hours dragged on, and Rachel wished Brandon would regain consciousness. It was selfish, she knew, but she didn't want to face this alone. Removing his flak jacket, she set it on the floor beside him. Shivering more from fear than cold, she resumed her spot next to him. Noticing something inside his shirt pocket, she undid the button and removed a small book. Taking it over to the little window that allowed in a sliver of moonlight, she held the cover up. *The Book of Mormon.* "Brandon Shepherd is a Mormon?" she muttered. Looking at the unconscious man, she smiled and shook her head. *Well,* she thought, *that explains a few things.* She checked his vitals one more time and brushed her fingers across his forehead. Sitting down next to him, she turned the book over in her hands, debating in her mind. Realizing she had nothing but time on her hands, she finally stood and went back over to the window. Opening the cover, she held it up so she could see better as she leaned against the wall and began to read.

* * *

When Brandon came to, the room was beginning to get light, and from the amount of light coming through the tiny window, he surmised it was early morning. He tried to sit up but sank back down. "Rachel?"

Rachel guided his head back down into her lap. "Shh. I'm here. Just be still." She lightly stroked the stubble on his cheek; she looked relieved he was awake. Then she took his wrist to feel for his pulse. "You've been unconscious for quite a while. Just take things slow."

He lay back down, feeling exhausted. "It must have been that concussion from earlier."

She only nodded and continued with his pulse. "Your vitals seem steady and strong," she said finally.

"Did you get any sleep?" he asked, noting the dark circles under her eyes. "Has anyone come in?"

"Yes, I slept a little," she told him. "And no, it's just been you and me."

"And I wasted our time together being unconscious?" He gave a small smile. "I won't let that happen again." He felt lighter somehow. When he reached for his flak jacket, he realized that Rachel must have taken it off. He also noticed that the familiar bump in his shirt pocket, where the Book of Mormon should have been wasn't there anymore.

"Are you looking for this?" Rachel asked, holding up his tiny book.

"Yes," he said, relieved.

"While you were unconscious I took a closer look at it. I didn't know you were Mormon," she said, raising one eyebrow. "And a Mormon who can hot-wire a car no less."

"Well, I recently became one, actually." Brandon looked at her, his expression serious. "Right before my deployment. " He tried to gauge her reaction.

She smiled. "One of my professors was a Mormon. I always admired her work ethic."

"Her work ethic?" Brandon laughed. "I can see that about you. I'll bet you admire punctual people, too."

She turned away. "There's nothing wrong with that."

Brandon wanted to reach up and touch her face, but he resisted. "I know. I'm just teasing you." He sat up slowly, leaning against the wall. "So, do you have a church that you attend?"

"No. I never had time for religion or anything else after I got out of medical school."

"Yeah, me neither. Until now." He looked at the book in his hand. "So how much of it did you read?"

Before she could answer, the door flew open and a guard strode into the room. He didn't say a word, just grabbed Rachel by the arm, hauling her against his side. "Come," he growled.

Brandon tried to intervene, standing up and positioning himself between the guard and the door. "Where are you taking her?" he demanded.

The guard pushed him back. "She is to be questioned."

Shaking his head, Brandon firmly took Rachel's other arm. "No. We stick together."

The guard pointed his gun at Brandon, but his face showed no anger. "I do not wish to hurt you."

Brandon took a step. "Go ahead. You're not taking her anywhere."

Rachel intervened as the two men squared off, standing almost toe to toe. "Brandon, don't. One of us has got to make it out of here alive."

Brandon stepped slightly away and stood close to her, bending his head to hers. "We're both going to make it out of this. You stay strong, remember? No matter what." He touched her shoulder with what he hoped was an encouraging gesture.

The guard sneered. "I'll be back for you." Holding Rachel's arm tightly, he escorted her to the door. She looked back and gave Brandon a shaky smile. "See you soon," she mouthed.

When she was gone, Brandon kicked the wall in frustration. What would they do to her? He felt helpless. Dropping to his knees, he began to pray.

* * *

Rachel was led down a long corridor at the end of which was a large bedroom. Taking a deep breath, she stepped in. Mofak Jassem was there waiting for her, and another man was sitting to his left near a large dresser. "Come in," Mofak said. "Sit down."

Rachel did as she was told, adjusting the abayah as she sat down.

Mofak came to stand over her. He was silent for a moment, running his finger down his jaw as if he were thinking. Rachel noticed a slight scar on his cheek, just below his eye, and wondered how he'd gotten it. She glanced at his eyes and saw that he was watching her intently; her stomach twisted in fear as he touched the scar she'd been staring at. "Tell me how long you have practiced medicine." His voice was low and menacing, and his eyes never left hers.

"I've been in school for several years and stationed with the army for two years." Her breath was coming in tiny gasps from fear; she bent her head as she answered, breaking eye contact and trying to appear respectful.

"How much are you told about military operations near al-Qaim?" he asked.

"I'm not privy to that information," she replied, taking a deep breath to calm her racing heart.

Mofak squatted in front of her, forcing her to look at him. "I want the truth from you. I do not want to make you suffer. Did you know about any covert operations or military advances near the border of Syria?"

Rachel again looked him directly in the eyes, willing herself not to turn away from the darkness she saw in his soul. "I was not privy to any military information," she repeated, hearing the desperation creep into her voice. "I am a doctor. I heal people."

"And that will be providential for us," he responded before standing. "We needed a doctor, and one was provided. Allah Akbar." He motioned for the guard to come forward. "Take her upstairs."

Rachel breathed a sigh of relief at the questioning being over but felt a spike of fear as she wondered what was upstairs. She pushed down the panic, taking slight comfort in the knowledge that they apparently needed her medical skills; she knew that this was probably the only thing keeping her alive right now. She pulled her abayah closer around her and stood before the men as they led her out of the room.

* * *

Brandon sat quietly, trying to calm the adrenaline rushing through his body and trying not let his thoughts wander too far. He had paced until he was dizzy and had finally settled on counting all the cracks in the ceiling. All the while he prayed that Rachel was all right. Suddenly, the door was thrust open, and two guards came into the room.

They hauled Brandon to his feet, and he fought off a wave of nausea as he tried to appear steady. "Mofak is ready," one guard said.

He was led upstairs through a maze of hallways to a back bedroom. Rachel was standing in front of the door with another guard; it looked like they'd been waiting for him.

"Rachel!" Brandon exclaimed. "Are you all right?"

Rachel nodded and received a hard look from her guard. Brandon felt light-headed with relief. They stood in front of a doorway for a few moments as Rachel's abayah was repositioned by the guard. When she was fully covered, he opened the door, and they were ushered into the room. Brandon looked around at a lavishly decorated bedroom. There was a large, four-poster bed in the middle and luxurious rugs covering the floor. A bearded man was lying in the bed, his deathly white face a contrast with his dark brown beard. Mofak Jassem stood facing the man but turned when Brandon and Rachel approached.

"This is Sayed Fahim," he said quietly, almost reverently, as he held his hand toward the man lying in the bed. "He is in need of medical attention."

Neither Rachel nor Brandon moved after Mofak announced the patient's name. It was as if they were frozen in disbelief. They were standing in the presence of one of the world's most notorious terrorists. The United States had been hunting Sayed due to his role in large-scale attacks all over the world—attacks that often targeted Americans.

Mofak smiled. "You recognize his great name, I see. This is providential. I have brought you here to save the man that has killed many Americans as he fought in our jihad against your country and what it stands for."

"You can't be serious," Rachel said, shaking her head, her expression angry. "How can you expect us to help someone who has killed our countrymen?"

Mofak looked at Brandon, raising an eyebrow. "Is that what you say as well?"

Brandon stood motionless for a moment, then looked over at Rachel. Their eyes locked. When he looked away and moved toward the bed, Rachel gasped. "Brandon, no!"

"Rachel, we're doctors, and there is a critically wounded patient in front of us." Brandon willed her to understand. "We can't let him die."

"Did *he* care when innocent Americans were dying?" she protested. "Do you know how many people have lost their lives just searching for this man?"

Mofak smiled and nodded as if enjoying their argument. He discreetly turned to inspect some large cables on the floor running into a closed doorway. Rachel leaned in closer to Brandon. "If we let him die, we could save *American* lives."

"I can't sit back and let a man die when there's a chance I could save him," Brandon said firmly. "That would be murder to me."

"But he's a murderer!" she whispered, her voice taut and angry. "He's going to murder again—probably more Americans—and if you save him, their deaths would be on your head!"

"Rachel, I know this is hard for you to understand, but my religion teaches that there is life after death and that we will be judged for our actions. I believe these things. This man will answer to God for his actions, just as I will answer to God for mine. I won't have this man's death on my head." He looked down at the patient and started to pull back the covers.

"You don't make any sense." Rachel clenched her teeth. "How can you stand there in your military uniform and say you'll help this man?"

He watched her step away from him, carefully maneuvering so as to keep her abayah from shifting. He sympathized with her conflicting emotions. He knew exactly how she was feeling, but he could not turn against his personal beliefs. "I am a patriotic American," he said, looking her in the eye. "I love my country, and I would gladly give my life for the cause of freedom. I know what you're feeling, because I'm horrified too. And then there's the possibility that no matter what we do, he'll die anyway."

At these last words, Mofak stepped up behind them. "If he dies, you both die as well," he stated matter-of-factly. "The cameras will be ready so we can show the world that Americans have saved a man they say they hate and would do anything to capture dead or alive. Surely you know there is a large bounty on the head of Sayed Fahim. Isn't it ironic that you will save the man your government would pay millions of dollars to have in their custody? Money like that would change your lives forever. Your saving this man's life will change it as well. But will it be for the better or worse?" His voice had gotten softer as he spoke, and his eyes glittered.

Rachel shook her head. "I won't have anything to do with this. I'd rather die than help that man."

The guard started to raise his gun toward Rachel, and Brandon felt a surge of panic. Holding up his hand, he addressed Rachel but looked pointedly at Mofak. "Rachel, I can't do this alone, I need you. Please."

Rachel looked at the guns raised toward her, and her bravado seemed to lessen. She didn't say she would help, but she moved closer to the bed. Brandon sighed with relief. "What happened to him?" he asked Mofak.

"There is a bullet and some shrapnel lodged in both his shoulder and his chest," Mofak explained. "The Americans almost caught us coming over the Syrian border. I need him ready to travel in five days, no longer."

Brandon didn't respond and slowly uncovered Sayed Fahim's torso. Pulling back the crude bandages, he inspected the shoulder injury. Nodding to himself, he then looked at the chest trauma. Carefully exploring the entrance wounds, he looked at Fahim's back as best he could, then finished and stepped back. "The shoulder wound is superficial and will be easy to fix. The chest wound, however, is more complicated. There is no exit wound, and I think the bullet must be very near the heart. If he doesn't have surgery, there could be blood clots or the bullet could travel to the heart. Anything could happen, and all the scenarios are bad and potentially lethal."

"Then you will operate," Mofak declared.

"It's not as simple as that," Brandon shot back. "He needs to be in a hospital. Perhaps in Baghdad—"

Mofak cut him off. "You will do the surgery here, and you will keep him alive. Otherwise you will die."

"Even if we do save him," Brandon continued, "he won't be ready to travel in five days. He has a long recovery ahead of him."

Mofak sneered. "You have no idea who you're dealing with, do you? This is Sayed Fahim. He is a great leader, and the great Satan will never keep him down. He will be ready to travel in five days, because we have a great mission to fulfill." Pointing his finger at Brandon, Mofak smiled. "And you will help him and show the world your cowardice. Perhaps you will join us after you realize how great a cause this truly is."

"We will need supplies and a sterile place to work in," Brandon said, not bothering to address Mofak's final comment. Looking over at Rachel, he nodded. "I'll also need her expertise for the surgery. It's going to be complicated."

Mofak agreed. "You will be taken to the next room until all the preparations are made."

The guard stepped forward. Brandon quickly asked, "May we have a moment to wash? It wouldn't do any good to save Fahim if he dies from an infection afterward. We need to at least wash."

After thinking for a moment, Mofak motioned to the guard. "Yes. But you will be watched at all times. We cannot afford to have any more escape attempts. We are on a strict timetable."

"Thank you," Brandon said as he followed the guard down the hall to a bathroom. He stepped aside to let Rachel enter, but the guard stopped him and started to go in after Rachel. "She's a lady. She needs privacy," Brandon protested.

The guard looked confused for a moment, then finally nodded. Brandon waited outside with the guard while Rachel went inside. After a few moments she emerged, the blood washed off her face and hands. Then Brandon went in. Conscious of the fact that Rachel was outside with the guard alone, he hurried, using the bathroom and splashing water from the tiny trickle coming from the faucet onto his hands, face, and neck. After he had rejoined Rachel, he was led to the room next to Sayed's bedroom. Hearing the door lock behind them, Brandon leaned against the wall and massaged his neck.

"You *cannot* do this surgery. We have to make sure this man does not live through it," Rachel said. "Surely you understand that. He's Abu al-Masri's right-hand man. The fact that he's here means that something big is going down. Bin Laden can't be far behind. We would be helping them."

"Didn't you take an oath to do no harm?" Brandon asked her. "I don't remember it saying 'do no harm to only good people,' or 'do no harm to the people that you like.' It's just 'do no harm,' and it's an oath. I saw the compassion you felt for little Yusuf. I know you have it in you." He briefly closed his eyes. "My religion means a lot to me," he said softly. "I know you don't understand, but I believe I'll be held accountable for this man's life."

Rachel looked at him, confusion on her face. "But you saw the twin towers fall," she whispered. "You know what this man is capable of."

"We don't exactly have a lot of options," he reminded her. "If we don't save him, we'll be killed ourselves. Are you ready to die for revenge?"

She lowered her head and closed her eyes. "I understand what you're saying, Brandon. I just never thought I'd be in this position. I wish we could signal our whereabouts and have the military take this decision out of our hands."

He sank to the floor. "Me too. That would definitely solve a lot of our problems."

Rachel took off her head covering, brushed back her hair, and looked around their small room. "I don't think we'll be escaping from here with only that little window and a guard outside the door. Do you have any other ideas?"

"Not really," Brandon said. "I think we're halfway between Fallujah and al-Qaim; if they use that tape they made of us earlier, people will be searching." He tried to keep his voice matter-of-fact.

"Too bad we can't signal the searchers somehow—start a fire big enough to be seen. You're not carrying any matches, are you?" She gave a small laugh as Brandon shook his head. "That would have been too *providential,*" she said, mimicking Mofak's use of the word. "Are we really going to try to save one of the world's most wanted terrorists? On camera?" Rachel asked, still disbelieving the situation they were in.

"I think we have to." Brandon replied and began pacing the small room.

* * *

It had been thirty minutes since the guards had left them. Rachel knew that Brandon was warring within himself. She understood that he needed to stand by his beliefs, but she knew it was a tough choice for him to make. If they did make it out of this alive, how would they explain their actions? It seemed they would be hated—or worse—no matter what they did.

"What do you think is going on here?" she asked, watching him pace for a moment before grabbing his hand and pulling him to sit next to her on the floor. "Stop pacing. You're making me dizzy. Mofak kept talking about a timetable they're on. Do you think they're planning something in Iraq or abroad?"

"If I remember correctly, the security summit takes place in five days."

"The security summit," Rachel breathed. "Of course. It would be the perfect time for a terrorist attack. Representatives from the United States, Britain, Syria, and Iran will be meeting with the Iraqi government. It would undermine the very thing Americans are trying to assure the people of Iraq that they can achieve—security."

"That's probably why there was so much activity near al-Qaim. The military probably knew these guys were coming across and were waiting for them," Brandon mused. "I wonder how they got through."

"And how they managed to kidnap us in the process. How did they know we'd be coming?" She thought for a moment. "Where do you think Nazir fits into this whole thing? I don't think it's a coincidence he was at the place where the trucks had been attacked at the same time we were there."

Brandon looked at her. "No, I don't think it was a coincidence either. He was there when the chopper's destination was announced, remember? He knew where we were going. I'm sorry, Rachel, I know you really liked Nazir."

Rachel sighed. "I have a hard time believing he would betray us. I've worked with him on several humanitarian missions since I came here. He's a wonderful interpreter. He often spoke of his family and how much he enjoyed his work."

"Well, we don't know what his motives were. People are being kidnapped and ransomed every day. The tribes are feuding, the country is in chaos—nothing is certain. Brandon's stomach rumbled. "I wish we'd had something more to eat before we left."

Rachel gave him a small smile and gave a little laugh a few moments later as her own stomach rumbled. "I'm glad you're here," she said. "I don't know what I would have done if I'd actually come alone."

He smiled back at her. "I'm glad I came too. I bet the search for us is already underway. We'll be rescued before we know it."

"I know," she said softly. They both turned as the door creaked open.

"You will come now," the guard said, pointing his gun at them and flicking it in the direction they were to go.

Rachel and Brandon scrambled to their feet, and Rachel put on the head covering. Brandon was secretly grateful she was required to wear the abayah because of the protection it gave her from the guards' prying eyes. They followed their guard back to the bedroom where Sayed had been, only this time they were led through the room to a small, secret hallway which led to another wing of the house. They were pushed into a large area which was practically bare except for a cot in the middle. The medical supply cases that had been near the helicopter were placed strategically around the cot. Several bowls full of water were nearby, and Mofak stood near Sayed's bedside, which was surrounded by bright lights and the camera.

"We have everything you need," Mofak said to Brandon. "We have given Sayed a powerful sedative, so you may begin."

Brandon washed his hands again in one of the bowls of water, and Rachel did the same. They went to the bedside, and Brandon started setting out the instruments. "Have you performed surgeries like this before?" Brandon asked Rachel. "In the field?"

"No. I've observed several and assisted on two heart surgeries, though," she told him. "What about you?"

"This looks a little more complicated than the ones I've done, but I think we'll be okay," he said. "Just follow my lead. We'll do the best we can. I think we should tackle the shoulder wound first."

* * *

Rachel watched him set out the tools, sanitizing them as best he could. She admired how adeptly his long fingers handled the instruments. He definitely had a surgeon's hands. He was gentle with the patient as he pulled the bandage back and inspected the wound.

Mofak watched Brandon carefully, then turned and spoke into the camera. "As you can see, your American doctors are working hard to save Sayed Fahim, one of your most wanted. It would be considered an act of treason to aid and abet the enemy, would it not?" He laughed. "They will save him to save themselves because they are cowards!"

Brandon rolled his eyes and handed Rachel the gauze. She stifled a small smile.

"I'm going to remove the shrapnel, and I'll need you to keep the surgical path clear so I can see any fragments. Then I'll do the same for you," Brandon stated. She nodded, and he wiped his brow on his sleeve before he proceeded to remove the major fragments from the wound. The room was silent as the doctors worked, the only sound the buzzing of the lights.

"I think we've got them all," Rachel said, feeling a bead of sweat traveling down her back. She wanted to rip the abayah off, feeling like the black fabric was stifling her. Triumphantly bringing out the last fragment from the shoulder, she put it in a bowl, and it clanked as it hit the bottom. "Let's just double-check that there are no loose fragments left."

Brandon smiled at her. "You did great," he said, nodding before going back to work.

Rachel smiled to herself at his comment. Not because he'd complimented her, but because she knew he'd recognized what a difficult time she'd had trying to operate under the weight of her conscience. Turning back to her patient and the task before her, she finished her search for loose fragments and waited until Brandon had done the same. When both doctors were satisfied that there were no more fragments left inside Fahim, Brandon started to close the wound.

"Brandon, look," Rachel said, nodding her head toward Sayed. His face had turned a deathly gray.

Brandon felt for a heartbeat. "We're losing him," he said frantically. He immediately started compressions. "Come on, Sayed," he breathed. "Stay with us."

Mofak stopped Brandon's compressions and looked him straight in the eye. "Remember, if he dies, you die."

Brandon pushed Mofak's hand away. "Then let me do my job!" He continued the compressions. "Do we have anything to open his airway?"

Rachel reached into the supplies and pulled out a sterile package. "Aren't you glad I memorized where everything was?" she said grimly.

"Come on," Brandon said as he tried to restart Sayed's heart. "Don't die on me now!" Mofak called in the guard, and they both drew their weapons, training them on Brandon and Rachel. Rachel looked at Brandon, anticipating what was about to happen. No matter what happened, she knew this moment would be burned into their memories forever.

CHAPTER 8

Kristen twisted in her chair. The picture of her and Ryan in the newspaper this morning was generating a lot of interest. Her phone had been ringing off the hook. She had been careful to avoid the questions about her relationship with Ryan but had taken the opportunity to discuss Xavier Addison's ethics in the political arena and the fact that his reputation as a philanthropist was above reproach. It was an old spin tactic but useful. Jack was an expert at it and had told her that if she had the ear of the press, she had to use her time wisely. He was known in the business as the ultimate spin doctor. It was said Jack Pierson could put a positive spin on anything; it had earned him the nickname "The Top." Of course, no one called him that to his face.

Kristen took one more look at the picture. Ryan looked so annoyed; it was funny, really. He was such an easygoing person. *People can change,* she reminded herself. *I did.* Her cell phone rang, and she picked it up. "Hello, Kristen Shepherd."

"Ms. Shepherd, this is Agent Lewis from the Department of Homeland Security. I was wondering if I might come to Boston tomorrow and ask you a few questions."

Kristen switched the phone to her other ear and quickly got a pen and pad of paper out. "Agent Lewis? What does Homeland Security want with me?"

"I just need an appointment time, Ms. Shepherd." His tone was brusque and professional.

Kristen tapped her pen. "I have a debate tomorrow, but I could probably meet with you after that," Kristen said. "Should I get a lawyer?"

"I don't imagine you'll need one." He paused, and she heard him shuffling some papers.

Her mind buzzed with questions. "Tell me what this is about."

"Ms. Shepherd, I cannot comment on that at this time, but if I have any further questions or if I am given permission to give you any more information before we meet, I will contact you again. I will plan on seeing you tomorrow after the debate. What time is convenient and where would you like to meet?"

Kristen gave him the details. "Can you at least give me an idea of what I should expect?"

"Unfortunately, no. You may reach me at this number, but as I said, I won't be able to give you any additional information until our meeting." He rattled off the contact numbers, and Kristen quickly wrote them down. "Thank you again, and have a nice day."

Kristen rolled her eyes at his formality, then clicked off her phone, her mind racing. Should she get a lawyer? What could they possibly want? Before she could think on the matter any further, her phone rang again. She absently picked it up. "Kristen Shepherd."

"Kristen, it's Michael. I've been trying to get through for an hour," he sounded like a petulant child, and it irritated her.

"I've been busy with the press all morning," she said bluntly. "What can I do for you?"

"Were you talking to the press about your picture in the paper this morning? What were you doing at dinner with him?" Michael asked. "If it was business, I should have been there."

"It wasn't a business dinner," Kristen said. "He's an old friend." She stretched her neck, feeling tension creep across her shoulders. "Is that what you're calling about?"

Michael was silent for a moment, and Kristen knew he wanted to say something more. She heard him sigh, then say, "What time are you coming down to campaign headquarters? The first poll numbers should be coming in this afternoon, and we've got a strategy session with Xavier for the debate tomorrow."

"I'll be there. I'm on my way now. See you later." She ended the call. It wasn't easy working with him right now, but there was nothing to be done about it. She'd been putting off their confrontation, and she knew she needed to get it over with. Squaring her shoulders, she made a decision and began riffling through her file folder for the number to the bank in Saudi Arabia. Dialing the direct number she'd tracked down for the bank's manager, she was surprised that someone answered after only two rings.

"As-salam alaikum," he said quickly. "This is Mr. Azir. How may I help you?"

"Hello, this is Kristen Shepherd, Mr. Azir. I'm hoping you can help me. There was an unauthorized transfer attempt made from my bank accounts here in America to your bank in Saudi Arabia. I wondered if you would be able to tell me anything about that?"

She could hear a computer keyboard tapping in the background. "What is your name?" he asked.

"Kristen Shepherd."

"And when was the transfer made?"

She told him. There was silence on the other end. "Mr. Azir, are you still there?"

"Yes, madam. I'm afraid I can't help you. I'm very sorry." He was quiet, then added, "I would advise you to protect yourself and your finances from any more outside sources. It is a very dangerous world we live in, no?"

"Dangerous? What do you mean?" But before she'd even gotten the words out, all that sounded in her ear was the dial tone. Kristen hung up, perplexed. What was this all about?

She closed her eyes for a moment, then, more determined than ever in her resolve to figure things out, she dialed her own bank's number.

After asking specifically for the teller she'd talked to on her almost-wedding day, she was transferred. "Robyn, this is Kristen Shepherd. I was wondering if you had time for a few more questions."

"Certainly, Ms. Shepherd." She paused. "I'm really sorry about what happened."

"Thanks. Can you tell me again exactly what happened last Friday?" Kristen noticed she was tapping her pen nervously on the side table and stopped. It was a habit she was trying to break. In politics you couldn't give anything away, so she had to be especially careful about such things.

"Well, Mr. Forbes came in and said that all your bank accounts would be moving to the Al-Rajhi Bank in Saudi Arabia. He produced a letter that stated he had the legal authority to act for you, so we began the transfer. I only called you to verify the final arrangements."

Kristen's breath came faster as Robyn recited the rest of the details to her again. It was just too incredible to imagine. Yet, when she'd confronted Michael, he'd claimed he was only thinking of the future, that he could explain it to her, and that he couldn't imagine why she wouldn't trust him.

"Did you look at the papers carefully?" she asked the bank teller.

"Of course. They all seemed to be in order. Do you need to speak to my bank manager? He's taken over the case now."

"No, not right now. I'm just trying to sort out everything with the man who claimed to have my power of attorney. I'll let you know, though. And thank you."

"I just want you to know that we take fraud very seriously, Ms. Shepherd, and we're anxious to get this all sorted out."

"Thank you, Robyn. Do you have all my contact information so you can get back to me if you hear anything more or need to get in touch with me?" Robyn said she did, and Kristen thanked her again before ending the call. It just didn't make sense. What was Michael doing? And what danger was Mr. Azir talking about? Rubbing her temples, Kristen tried to gather her thoughts. It seemed that she wouldn't be finding more answers until she hashed this out with Michael. For her own peace of mind, she needed to have that conversation with him. It was shaping up to be one of those kind of days. Picking up her cell phone, she put in one last call to the State Department to see if she could talk to the diplomat Michael had served under. Perhaps he would have some answers for her.

After speaking with a diplomatic assistant and getting the promise of a callback, Kristen pulled herself together and headed for Xavier Addison's campaign headquarters. She smoothed her skirt, feeling good in her power jacket as she walked to the back room. As she opened the door, all eyes turned to her. Xavier Addison got up from his chair first and came to greet her. He was a handsome man, in his late fifties, Kristen guessed. His silver hair was combed back neatly, his blue eyes were sharp and clear, and he looked at her as if he were assessing her character. "Kristen," he said as he stretched out his hand, "I'm so glad you're here."

Michael pulled out a chair for her. "We didn't start without you, so don't worry."

Kristen took a deep breath and put on a smile. "I wasn't worried, Michael." She sat down and opened her briefcase, taking out several files. John Devine, one of Xavier's key strategists before her team had been called in, gave her a nod but didn't say anything. Kristen felt a simmering hostility emanating from him but decided to ignore it. She addressed the crowd. "Gentlemen, if Mr. Addison is going to win, we can't relax at all. We need to strengthen our platform and make this campaign memorable to the Massachusetts public."

"I would think I'm already memorable from my charity work," Xavier said, looking around the table.

"We want more than that," Kristen replied. "We want them to remember your ideas, what you will do for them. I think you need to focus on the three E's: education, economy, and environment. You'll hit a lot of people within those parameters."

"What are you suggesting, Kristen?" Michael asked.

"I'm suggesting that when he goes out to campaign, or when he does any PR, that he hit those three platforms again and again. Make it memorable." Kristen went into campaign mode, sitting back in her chair. "From what I can gather, that's what has been missing up until this point. You didn't have a focus, a message that resonated with Massachusetts voters. Let's change that. What do you think about Massachusetts's economy?" she asked Xavier.

"I think we have to carefully plan because of the growth we've been experiencing in this state. We can't just throw money at the problem; we have to have accountability and solutions," he said.

"Excellent." Kristen leaned forward and scribbled on her legal pad. "What is it about the economy that needs fixing?"

"Massachusetts could use some PR work to attract a larger tourism industry, and we could work at maintaining better balanced budgets, but overall I think we're doing okay."

"No," Kristen said. "We're never doing okay. In a campaign, we want voters to remember that you can make their lives better. The man who's out of work won't vote for you if you're telling him you think everything is okay. You need to step up to the plate and tell the public you're aware of their problems and that you're the man to help them—that you're someone they can count on." She wrote a few more notes. "Okay, what about the environment?"

"We want it protected, of course." Xavier was shifting uncomfortably in his seat.

"How are you going to make that meaningful to the voters?" Kristen asked.

Xavier shrugged. "I don't know."

"You're going to talk about Washington and tell them that you're the man who will work with them. You are someone the public can trust to make sure Massachusetts is safe for their children and their grandchildren. You make it count on their level."

Xavier leaned back in his chair and turned to John Devine. "This is what I mean. This is what we've needed all along. We just needed a little focus and redirection."

John's only response was to nod and keep staring at Kristen. He was making her uncomfortable, but she didn't show it.

"There's no time to waste," Kristen continued. "Up until this point, you haven't been connecting with the public. We need you out there on the trail to fix that and make the next six weeks count. Are we ready for the debate tomorrow?"

"Yes, we've been working hard on that," Xavier informed her.

"Great. What's your airtime been on radio and TV?"

"We've had quite a bit of airtime," Xavier said.

"Well, you must not have been using it wisely," Kristen said. "Especially if these poll numbers are right." She passed out a paper she'd picked up on the way over. "The public is drawn to Cameron Mitchell because he's a dynamic speaker. He gets more press. We need to make your profile higher and get these numbers up."

Michael laughed somewhat nervously. "She's got a jugular instinct," he said to the others in the room. "But we all know that the numbers aren't Xavier's fault."

Kristen turned to him, arching an eyebrow. "Whose fault are they, Michael?"

"His former management team, of course," Michael said. "He was taking bad advice."

At that comment, John got up and left the room. Xavier looked nonplussed. "John's a little sensitive right now. He thinks if he had a little more time, he could have turned things around. He didn't want to have any outsiders brought in," Xavier said apologetically. "Don't worry, I'll talk to him." He excused himself and went after John.

"What are you doing?" Michael said to Kristen as soon as the door closed.

"I'm doing my job," Kristen snapped back. "And I don't like being questioned in front of my client." She stood, and he moved to stand in front of her.

"That wasn't what I was doing, honey," he said, taking her arm.

She pulled away. "Don't call me honey, and that was exactly what you were doing."

"I don't want you to come across as too aggressive, that's all."

"Aggressive wins elections, Michael. You know that."

"I know that's not who you are on the inside." He caressed her hand, but she drew it back.

"Until I have some satisfactory answers as to why you tried to trick my bank into transfering all my money to a Saudi Arabian bank, I don't know what to believe about you or me or anything right now," Kristen countered.

Michael backed up a little. "Why don't you let me explain?"

Kristen nodded, and he continued, lowering his voice. "You know I served in Saudi Arabia as a diplomatic aide and that I was married to a girl there." He paused to look around, making sure no one was listening. "She was involved in a group that her older brother had started, and I attended some meetings with her. It seemed harmless enough, and I even went to some protests with them. But then the group started to get more militant and more radical. I tried to talk Madj out of it, but her brother has a tremendous hold on her. We ended up divorcing, and her brother was enraged. It got ugly, Kristen." Michael stepped closer to her. "I am a Forbes. When the group was listed on a terrorism watch list, I knew I couldn't be associated with them. I distanced myself as much as I could and divorced Madj, but I was blackmailed by Madj's brother. I paid for his silence to protect my family and their reputation. I wanted to protect you, too."

Kristen folded her arms. "You were trying to protect me by keeping silent about a big part of your life—one that apparently required you to steal from me?"

Michael looked down. "I just need you to understand that I was being blackmailed. They have pictures and evidence of my involvement in the group, and I had nowhere else to turn. I felt like the most prudent thing to do was to keep my actions well hidden and quiet to protect everyone that I love. I'm so sorry." He reached out to touch her arm, but she drew back.

"What happened when you didn't get my money?" Kristen asked, trying to read his expression. He didn't answer, and she saw a flash of guilt flicker across his face. "Are you telling me the truth?"

"Yes," he said quickly. "You have to believe me. I want to be with you. We're so good together."

Kristen looked at him, no longer seeing the man she'd once loved. "Have you stolen funds before?"

"I wasn't stealing from you, Kristen; I planned to pay you back. We were about to be married."

"And you didn't trust me!" she said, raising her voice. "How could I ever trust you again?"

"I don't know what's going on in that head of yours," Michael said, his expression hardening. "I told you what happened. I was putting the past behind me, building a strong foundation for our life together. I thought you would understand. I was doing what I thought was best for us and for everyone else concerned. Why won't you believe me?"

She stepped closer to him. "This is fraud, Michael, and you *were* stealing from me."

Michael's face twisted in anger. His fingers, which had been caressing her moments ago, now bit into her arm. "I explained myself to you. Don't you have any compassion at all? I was doing what I thought was best." He bought his face very close to hers. "We belong together. You need me. Don't you remember what your life was like before you met me? Work was all you had. I gave you a future."

"I don't want that anymore, Michael, and you're hurting me. Let go," she said firmly, wrenching her arm away. "I hope this was worth your future. I'm pretty sure that if you're charged with fraud, your career will be over.

Michael let go of her arm but didn't move away. He just stared at her, his eyes flashing angrily, his mouth a hard line. "You will lose *your* career and everything you love, Kristen. Mark my words. You should have married me when you had the chance."

"On the contrary; I just narrowly missed making the biggest mistake of my life," she snapped. "And if one of us is going to lose their career, I can tell you it won't be me. I'm sure the police will be very interested in my case."

He leaned in so close she could feel his breath on her cheek. "Do you think I would risk my career or my reputation? I am a *Forbes!* Why do you think I used your accounts, Kristen? My tracks are covered, and you made it so easy. If you expose me, you expose yourself. I can claim innocence, and my family will back me up. Who do *you* have?"

Kristen was stunned into silence. It had never occurred to her that he would frame her for his wrongdoings. "You're despicable."

Michael took a new approach. "All you have to do is marry me, and this will all go away. We can still be good together; you know we can. I made a mistake when I was younger, but that's in the past now. The family we would have together would be a Forbes family— powerful, rich, and wanting for nothing. You could have everything you've ever wanted." His voice was cajoling, his features softened. What she once found charming and sweet about him now seemed fake and contrived.

"Michael, I don't think you have any idea what I really want. But I will tell you this. I would rather lose my career and everything I own than marry you. Because if I married you, I would lose my self-respect. And that means more to me than anything you could ever take from me." And with that, she turned on her heel and walked out. The cards were on the table now, and Kristen was uneasy about the hand she'd been dealt. What had he done? What would he do? She rubbed her shoulders, trying to clear her head and relieve the tension.

Michael's veiled threat echoed in her mind as she started to unload her laptop. She felt compelled to check all of her bank accounts one more time; then she began going over any campaigns she'd done with Michael in the past year with a fine-tooth comb. Even though she knew Jack was investigating, she wanted to cover all her bases. She needed to know exactly what she was dealing with. But before her laptop even booted up, she was distracted by an argument in the outer office between Xavier and John. She pursed her lips. It was good this was happening now. The sooner John was onboard, the better for everyone. She left her laptop on the desk and walked over to Steve Leedom—a tall, lanky intern—and handed him a bullet-point list. "Steve, I've been watching you, and I like your dedication. I want you to be in charge of our war room. You'll be our rapid-response team director."

Steve looked taken aback for a moment, then a crooked smile spread across his face. "Yes, ma'am. But do you think Mr. Devine will approve?"

"I don't intend on asking Mr. Devine's permission. I'm in charge now." Kristen smiled. "I need someone I can trust, and you're my man."

He looked at her solemnly and nodded his head. "You can count on me, Ms. Shepherd."

"Okay, the first thing we need to do is use Governor Mitchell's strength against him. We need to be clever operatives and use whatever weapons we have."

"But Mr. Addison wants to run a clean campaign," Steve protested.

"It will still be a clean campaign," Kristen assured him. "We're just going to let Governor Mitchell shoot himself in the foot, so to speak." She leaned forward. "Governor Mitchell has two speaking engagements tonight and three more tomorrow. I want you to TiVo them, and we'll see if we get anything we can use. The first thing we need is a commercial that shows Governor Mitchell as a man who reacts, not a man who acts. Then we can portray Xavier as the action candidate. For the next two days, we're going to be a certain breed of sleepless media junkies."

"You'll help me?" Steve asked.

"Every step of the way," Kristen answered.

* * *

Kristen had wheedled her way into getting a last-minute invitation to the evening's fundraiser for Governor Mitchell, and she was glad she had. She sat at a table in the back, keeping a low profile and watching the event with interest. Ryan was up on the stage with Governor Mitchell, and she could tell they were feeling confident. It made her smile. In politics, confidence was the kiss of death because it could all change on a dime. Looking around at the crowd, Kristen felt a rush of excitement wash over her. Governor Mitchell was going to need all the help he could get when she got through with him.

After a brief introduction, Governor Mitchell strode to the podium. She had to admit he had presence when he walked into a room. His brown hair was swept back, his dark blue suit was crisp and perfectly groomed, and, as always, he knew all the right hands to shake. Kristen listened as the governor started his speech with a joke and quickly went on to his main points. In the middle of his speech, however, a heckler near the front shouted out, "Why did you cut funding for veterans?"

Governor Mitchell continued without reacting to the comment, but the man persisted and asked again.

Kristen saw Ryan signal for security as the heckler advanced to the stage, still speaking loudly. Governor Mitchell turned and faced him head on. "I wanted more funding for our veterans," he explained, "but there were too many amendments tacked onto it, including a tax cut for the rich. I just couldn't do it."

The heckler stood, making quite a display in his army uniform, shaking his head at the governor as security approached. "You have dishonored our veterans."

The governor looked stunned. Security now surrounded the man, but the governor held up his hand. "Sir, my father was a veteran. I could never dishonor him. I wanted that funding to pass. In fact, I was the first to approve it, but I had to veto it due to the extra amendments. We'll get something cleaner passed—you mark my words."

Kristen watched carefully as the heckler was escorted out, and the speech went on as planned. *This is it. We have him.*

* * *

Thirty minutes before Kristen arrived at "Addison for Governor" headquarters, Steve Leedom had marked the moment in Governor

Mitchell's speech that had caused such a stir. He had been monitoring the war room, surrounded by three televisions and a battery of TiVos and VCRs, eating a Twinkie and fiddling with the remote controls. He marked a few other things she might be interested in, then sat down to wait.

As soon as he saw her, he pulled out everything he'd marked. "I think I have what you want," he told her, queuing up the tape. She watched and nodded in approval as Steve wound the clip back and copied it to a tape. She sat down at his computer. Within moments she had copied an instant rough transcript and had e-mailed it to an "alert list."

Before the e-mail had even finished uploading, Kristen was on the phone to her advertising team. "Jack, I just sent you the footage for our new ad," she said into the receiver. "Did you get it?"

She waited a few moments until he confirmed. "The greatest gifts in politics are the ones the other side gives you," she said, smiling as she hung up.

"What do we do now?" Steve asked.

"All we have to do is drop the footage of Governor Mitchell saying 'I wanted that veteran's funding to pass, and I was the first to approve it, before I had to veto it.' It makes him sound like he can't decide whether he wants to support our troops or not, and it will make a great ad. It'll be plastered all over the Internet by the end of the day." She shook her head and walked back to her desk, the adrenaline still pumping. There was something exciting about the battlefield of a campaign—and they had just drawn first blood.

CHAPTER 9

Kristen craned her neck to look around at the crowd that had gathered for the evening's debate. She couldn't believe the week she'd had. In a matter of days, she had broken an engagement because she believed her fiancé capable of fraud, moved back home, and joined a campaign that was moving full steam ahead—one that she felt she had a good chance of winning. It was both exhilarating and exhausting, but Kristen wouldn't have it any other way. Taking a deep breath, she closed her eyes. If she slowed down at all, she'd have time to think of her personal problems, and she wasn't ready for that. Not yet. She knew she was going to have to face the problems sometime. She just couldn't face them tonight.

Camera crews were setting up, the panel was ready, and the butterflies were stirring in her stomach. That's when she knew it was going to be good. She went to stand beside Xavier, who was fixing his tie. "Are we set?"

He patted her arm. "As ready as we'll ever be. Thanks for helping me do this tonight. I feel more confident having you on my team. It's amazing what you've been able to do in only a few days."

"Just remember what we talked about. Stay calm and drive home our three points. When the regular guy on the street identifies with you, you've got his ear." She smiled and glanced across the floor. The governor and his staff were just arriving, and Ryan was at the governor's elbow. He returned her smile with a little wave. He looked nervous, which only heightened Kristen's feeling that this was going to be a very good night.

She strode quickly to Michael, who had the final checklist. Coming up behind him, she looked over his shoulder. "Hey." He turned, greeting her, though his tone wasn't friendly.

"I want to make sure we've made all the final preparations for tonight," she said, backing up a little and smoothing her skirt. He stepped closer, but his smile didn't reach his eyes. He was still angry with her.

"We're ready," he reassured her, his jaw set.

Kristen was uncomfortable with how close he was standing but didn't want to show it. She smiled, trying to appear relaxed. "Okay, then. I'll go tell the moderator we're ready."

He took her arm before she could walk away. "Kristen, I think we should talk more about things. I don't think you really understand."

"Not tonight." She shook her head and pulled her arm away a little more roughly than she had intended. "Let's just get through this campaign, okay?" Their eyes locked, and for a split second she thought she saw hurt and fear in Michael's expression, and she felt her guard slipping. Squaring her shoulders, she stopped herself from feeling sorry for him. No matter what else had happened, he had betrayed her. She couldn't forget that.

She walked out and didn't look back, even though she could feel his eyes on her. Blowing out a breath, she shook her hands out in an effort to get rid of the butterflies she was feeling. She looked up and saw Ryan watching her. From the way he was standing, it was obvious that he'd seen the entire exchange with Michael. His fists were clenched as if he were ready to come and protect her. Smiling to herself that she could still read him, she shook her head and walked toward the stairs where the moderator, a small, rotund man named Rod Jensen, was waiting. Rod was a news anchor who'd agreed to moderate the evening. He had a reputation for fairness.

Kristen gave him her best smile as she approached. "Are you nervous, Rod?" she asked him, quickly striding to his side.

He threw his head back and laughed, making his bald head shine in the lights. Pushing his glasses back up on his nose, he said, "I've faced worse than this. I'm not nervous at all. How about you?"

At that moment, Ryan joined the two of them, straightening his tie. It was hard to ignore how well the cut of his suit accentuated his frame.

He'd always taken good care of himself, and it showed. Kristen looked up at him and he smiled at her. "Did I miss something?" he asked pleasantly.

"Not at all," Kristen said smoothly, dragging her mind back from its reflection on Ryan's appearance. "Are you ready for tonight?"

"Definitely. Are you ready?"

"I'm always ready," she assured him.

Rod chuckled. "You have a formidable opponent. It ought to be a good debate."

Kristen nodded and, turning away, began to walk back to the staging area. Ryan fell into step beside her. "Is everything okay?" he asked her, his smile fading. "Do you want me to go get your father? I saw him in the audience."

"What do you mean?" She didn't meet his eyes but just kept staring at the backstage technicians as they made all the last-minute adjustments.

"I saw you talking to Michael earlier, and it looked tense. I wondered if I ought to be defending your honor or something. Or maybe you want your father to back you up. I don't know, but it seems like that's the least I can do while Brandon's not here." He opened the side door for her, and she went through.

Her face clouded. "I wish he were here. He'd know the right thing to do."

"I'm a good listener if you ever need to talk," Ryan offered. "You can trust me."

Kristen hesitated for a second, hearing the sincerity in his voice. Maybe she should talk this out with someone and try to figure out what she should do. What if Michael made good on his threat to frame her? Ryan was an attorney; perhaps he could give her some advice. But before she could say anything, a photographer stepped in front of them and snapped their picture. She put on her practiced smile and simply said, "It's okay. I can take care of myself." She tried to sound reassuring, but he still looked worried.

"Do you have any comment before the debate begins?" the photographer asked, effectively cutting off any more personal conversation between Kristen and Ryan.

"No, I don't," Ryan said as he shook his head and smiled politely before moving to his part of the stage. "I'll see you in there," he said to Kristen as he walked away.

Kristen nodded and talked to the photographer briefly before rejoining her team. Part of her wished she'd had more time with Ryan. For that split second it felt like old times, when Ryan had been the safe haven she could always count on. She took one more look at him, surrounded by his campaign people, and shook her head. *Put that thought out of your mind,* she scolded herself.

Just then, her eyes fell on a laptop case near the stage, and she recognized the familiar engraved *F* on the side. Moving closer, she quickly picked it up, taking it offstage to a small corner behind the curtained area where she could open it. She knew this was probably the only chance she'd have to look at Michael's computer. Crossing her arms over her waist, she looked around; when she didn't see him anywhere, she opened it. Her personal research hadn't produced any clues; maybe this was her chance to find out what was going on. With his need for perfection he would have documented all of his transactions on his laptop since he was never without it. She waited for it to boot up, then began looking at the icons. Within minutes she was browsing through his documents. Clicking on his finance program, she skimmed through the normal files. Everything seemed to be in place—just like the files from her own laptop. She was about to close the programs she'd opened when she spied it. *A hidden file.* She clicked on the little ghost icon that was barely visible in the lower left-hand corner. The screen popped up, and a dialogue box asked for a four-letter password. As if she were being guided, she immediately thought of Michael's ex-wife, Madj. Typing in the name, the file opened before her. Kristen gasped. All the proof that Michael had committed corporate fraud was right in front of her. Bank accounts tied to Saudi Arabia and Iraq were meticulously documented, and her name was liberally sprinkled throughout.

"What are you doing?" Michael demanded, coming up behind her. He quickly snapped the computer shut. "And you accuse me of being dishonest! How much did you see?"

She backed up, her eyes wide, unable to believe what she'd just seen. "Why, Michael? Why would you do something like this? You stole from me *and* from the company," she said in shock.

"You obviously don't understand or you don't want to understand," he told her, looking around to see if anyone was close enough to hear their conversation. "I want you to, though. If you would just let me explain things, I know we could work this out."

Kristen ran her hands through her hair and realized she was shaking. She folded her arms, feeling completely bewildered by the man standing in front of her, someone she had once trusted and loved. "Okay, I'm listening."

Michael looked around again, then led her backstage and into a small, secluded hallway. He took her by the arm, as if afraid she would run, given the chance. He leaned closer, his voice low. "When I was in Saudi Arabia, the people that Madj and I met were powerful men with powerful allies. I didn't agree with their philosophies, and when I refused to associate with them anymore, they threatened to take my limited involvement and go public. I knew they would exaggerate my involvement, and, while I could probably prove that it was limited, the damage would be done. Could you imagine the headlines? My family wouldn't be able to show their faces. So I did what I had to do. I also knew that those men were dangerous and could do more than ruin my reputation. I know about them. I stood next to them."

"But you didn't agree with them?" Kristen asked quietly.

"Not really. They do have a vision of making the United States see that a free Iraq will not build the partnerships the Iraqis want in the Middle East. The leaders of this group want a *united* Iraq without a U.S. presence, and they don't care who they hurt or what they have to do to achieve it. They believe that people are like sheep and just need a little persuasion to go where a strong leader takes them. Sometimes I agree." He took her by the shoulders. "I ran into some unexpected snags because they needed the money sooner than I expected, that's all. I wanted to make this my final payment, but I was still trying to work out the details. I didn't have any choice but to use your money. I'm sorry. I wanted to tell you, but I didn't think you would understand. I didn't want to hurt you. I was going to explain everything as soon as we were married."

Kristen looked at him as if he'd suddenly lost his mind. "Are you telling me that you're being blackmailed into funding a terrorist group that is trying to make sure the Iraqi people never win their freedom? Didn't Saddam Hussein already try that? It didn't work, you know. People want to be free."

"I didn't know what else to do. Either I paid them or I lost everything." He looked down at the floor. "I had to do it, Kristen."

"How did I get involved? You used me to cover your tracks."

"I never would have hurt you, Kristen."

"You already did," she said sadly. "It's over, Michael."

"Don't say that," he told her. "I was being blackmailed. Surely you can understand. I needed the money."

"From what I saw on your laptop, you've needed quite a bit of money. You've been taking money that was meant to elect people in this country who would protect freedom and giving it to men who want to take freedom away. It's wrong, Michael, and you brought me into it. You said you were going to frame me!" Kristen's tone was incredulous. How could she have not seen this side of him?

"I'm a victim, too, Kristen. I think there's something big going on here. They want people to know what they're capable of; I think that's why they needed the money so quickly. I didn't know what to do. I only used your bank account as a last resort. And I used your name on some other transactions only when absolutely necessary. I wanted us to face this together."

She snorted. "None of this was necessary, and you are not a victim, Michael. You betrayed me and you know it. You should have gone to the authorities a long time ago."

He leaned forward, and from the look on his face, Kristen knew he was nearing the end of his rope. He opened his mouth to say something, then stepped back as they heard footsteps approaching. Ryan rounded the corner, obviously in a hurry, and almost bumped into them. "Kristen, there you are! Everyone's asking for you. We're about to start."

Kristen looked up at Ryan and knew he sensed that something was wrong, but she just shook her head. Michael's gaze implored her to understand him. She didn't.

"Can we talk about this later?" he asked, glancing at Ryan then back at her.

"I don't know, Michael. I don't think there's anything left to say," her voice was small, even to her own ears. She bit her lip, trying to get ahold of herself.

Michael reached out to her, but Kristen flinched and moved away. She needed time to think this through, and she definitely didn't want him touching her. Watching her reaction, Ryan stepped forward. "I'm not sure what's going on here, but Kristen obviously doesn't want to talk about it right now. Maybe we can all sit down after the debate," he suggested, placing himself firmly between Kristen and Michael.

"I don't think so," Michael shot back, drawing himself up to his full height. "This is between Kristen and me. In fact, I think you should leave."

"I'll leave when Kristen wants me to," Ryan retorted. Both men turned to Kristen.

She closed her eyes briefly. "Ryan, thank you, but I'm fine, and I think we should all go back in to the debate."

"Our discussion is not over," Michael stated. "We're going to finish this." He raised a finger to emphasize his point. "Remember, we're in this together—and you know I'm telling the truth about that." He glared at Ryan once more before walking away.

Kristen gave a nervous laugh, but Ryan wasn't fooled.

"Kristen, tell me what's going on. You're shaking like a leaf." He stepped closer to her and put his hand on her shoulder, his eyes full of concern. "That sounded like a veiled threat to me. Are you in trouble?"

She looked up at him and felt emotion rising in her chest. It was ironic, really. She had thought she couldn't trust Ryan, and she had thought she could trust Michael. But now everything seemed flip-flopped. "If anyone ever found out . . ." Kristen shivered slightly.

"You can trust me, Kristen. With anything. Let me help you."

Kristen closed her eyes, feeling the steady warmth of his arm around her shoulders. She felt her defenses cracking as her heart opened for the first time since the day of her wedding. "On my wedding day, I found out that Michael . . ." She stopped, trying to regain her composure when she felt the tears gathering in her eyes. But before she could say anything else, thunderous applause broke out. "Oh, Ryan, the debates have started. They're going to be looking for me." She stepped back and carefully wiped her eyes. "I have to go. I'm late."

He put his other arm around her and drew her into his embrace. She let herself be held for a moment, relishing the feeling of being safe and protected. When they broke apart, she felt bereft, as if a warm blanket had been suddenly yanked away.

"We'll talk after the debate," he promised. "We'll get to the bottom of this together."

Kristen gave him a shaky smile and felt better at his reassurance. It was like she'd suddenly been given a tiny ray of hope to lead her out of this mess.

* * *

Kristen stood in the wings, watching the debate. Xavier was doing well, holding his own and making her proud, but she couldn't get her mind off of what Michael had told her and the feelings Ryan had stirred in her. Steve Leedom appeared at her side, looking nervous. "Hey, Steve, isn't he doing great?" Kristen said.

Steve glanced at Xavier but then looked down. "Some men are here to see you and Michael. Do you know where he is?"

"What men?"

He pointed behind him. "That one says he's from Homeland Security; the other two say they're from the army." He twisted his tie in his hand, looking around before settling his gaze back on her.

Kristen felt the blood drain from her face, and for a moment she thought she was going to faint. Apparently Steve did too, because he took her arm. Frankly, she had forgotten about the Homeland Security appointment, but at least the visit was expected. The only thing you could expect from an official army visit when you had a serviceman in the field was bad news. "I'll be right there, Steve," she said, her voice a mere whisper.

At that moment a commotion began on the auditorium floor. Two men were struggling with Michael, apparently attempting to get him out of the room. Kristen hurried through the wings and down the steps, trying to get to the floor, but the press was blocking her way, snapping pictures. She doggedly pushed her way through just in time to see them burst through the back doors toward the lobby. Michael spotted her and yelled, "Remember what I said, Kristen. If I go down, you go down!" He jabbed his finger at her, obviously thinking that she had turned him in.

Within moments, microphones were pushed in her face. The questions came so fast, Kristen couldn't even make sense of them. All she could think of to say was "no comment" before she hurried away.

"Kristen, wait!" Ryan called to her. She turned around to see him and her father close on her heels. "What's going on?"

Her focus was on the uniformed men in front of her. They were standing to the side, but their presence alone made a scene. She slowed down and waited for Ryan and her father to catch up with her.

The men in military uniform hung back as a man in a suit approached her. He held out his hand. "Ma'am, I'm Agent Lewis. I spoke with you on the phone."

She shook his hand. "Yes, I was expecting you later tonight." Glancing at the other two men, she raised her eyebrows. "I didn't think you'd bring all these people. What's this all about?"

"We've had some new developments," he said as he glanced down the hallway where they'd taken Michael. "Is there someplace we could talk?"

At this point, one of the army men stepped forward, nodding to Kristen but addressing her father. "Aren't you General Grant Shepherd?"

Her father pursed his lips and glanced at Kristen before answering. Kristen could see the muscles in his jaw working. "Yes, I am."

Agent Lewis held up a hand as if he wanted the soldier to stop, but the soldier shook his head at the agent. "It's my duty, sir," he murmured.

With a small salute, the soldier continued. "Sir, I regret to inform you that your son, Captain Brandon Shepherd, is missing in action and presumed captured."

Kristen watched the shock harden her father's jaw; he didn't show any other reaction. She was finding it hard to concentrate with the sudden roaring in her ears. She felt Ryan reach for her arm, but she stepped away from him to stand in front of the officers. "What happened to my brother? Why do you think he's been captured? What do you know?"

The taller of the two spoke. "Unfortunately, ma'am, that's all the information we have at the moment."

Kristen let out a breath, and her shoulders sagged with relief at the one piece of potentially good news. "He's not dead," she said softly with relief. "He's not dead then."

The soldiers glanced at each other but didn't contradict her. Kristen walked a few steps to a lobby couch and sat down, her arms crossed over her stomach. She looked dazed. Ryan sidestepped the general and sat next to her, his hand on her back. "Kristen, are you all right?"

Before she could say anything, the Homeland Security agent came to stand in front of her. "Ms. Shepherd, I understand that finding out about your brother must come as a shock; however, I really do need to ask you some questions."

"What kind of questions?" Ryan asked. "This really isn't a good time."

She stood up. "I need to get home and call some of my contacts in Washington. Someone's got to know something more."

"Let me drive you," Ryan offered, standing with her and putting his hand on her arm to stop her from leaving.

"I'm sorry, but part of what I need to speak to you about involves your brother's capture." Agent Lewis glanced over at Kristen's father. "I should probably talk to both of you."

Kristen looked at her father, who nodded. "Okay, fine. I'm sure we can find an empty room somewhere."

Agent Lewis nodded. "Thank you."

"I'm coming with you," Ryan said. "You may need a lawyer."

"We'll all go," the soldier standing behind them suggested to Ryan. "Then you can wait outside for Ms. Shepherd. We've also brought along a chaplain if you'd like to talk to him." Kristen's father grunted but didn't comment. Kristen couldn't imagine him talking to anyone about feelings, least of all an army chaplain he didn't know. But then again, maybe he would be more comfortable with a stranger; she didn't really know. She'd never been privy to that side of her father.

Ryan was silently watching her, and she was grateful he didn't say anything more. General Shepherd and the two army representatives trailed behind Kristen and Ryan as they followed Agent Lewis. Kristen thought it was odd that everyone was coming, but she didn't say anything. Her mind was racing with the overload of information.

It looked like this had to do with Michael's being detained—was the government already aware of what he was doing? Was that why she was being questioned? What did this have to do with her brother?

"We need to make some phone calls," she said over her shoulder to her father.

"I know we do," he said quietly, but he gave her a look that said he didn't want to talk about it right then.

They finally reached an empty room, and Agent Lewis opened the door for Kristen. Ryan tried to follow her in, but Agent Lewis stopped him. "Ms. Shepherd doesn't need a lawyer."

Her father joined them and indicated that Ryan should come inside anyway. She'd seen that determined look on her father's face many times. "I think we all should stay together, don't you?" He stood toe to toe with Agent Lewis, not budging an inch.

The agent looked him in the eyes for several long moments, then finally stepped back and held his arm out. "After you, then."

Kristen played with the tiny gold necklace at her throat as she walked by the men and entered the room. It was small, with a lectern and a table pushed against the wall, and it had been set up with several chairs facing each other. Ryan and Agent Lewis took the seats across from her, and her father took the chair next to her.

"Okay, what do you need to ask me, and what does this have to do with my brother?" Kristen said, getting right to the point.

Agent Lewis didn't reply, but he took a laptop computer out of his briefcase. He went about setting it up. "What do you know about Michael Forbes's business dealings in Saudi Arabia, particularly financing a terrorist group?"

Kristen glanced at Ryan and saw his eyes widen. She didn't dare look at her father, so she just focused on the agent. "I know a little," she admitted. "I found out on my wedding day that he'd tried to have all the money in my bank accounts transferred to a Saudi Arabian bank."

The agent nodded. "Do you know why he would be giving money to them?" He folded his arms. "And did you know anything about this before your wedding day?"

Kristen looked down. "He said he's being blackmailed. I'm sure he can tell you all about it. And I didn't know anything until my bank called me on my wedding day." Her father mumbled something under his breath. Kristen immediately felt defensive. "I trusted him completely. I'd never had a reason not to trust him."

"When did you find out about the blackmail?" the agent asked quietly.

"We'd discussed it briefly the other day, but just before the debate tonight I got on Michael's computer and accessed some of his financial information. He caught me and told me in more detail about the blackmailing. It was quite an eye-opening conversation," she said with a hint of bitterness. "I just kept looking at him, wondering how I'd missed this side of him."

"You can't blame yourself, Ms. Shepherd. Did he happen to mention if he knew what the money was intended for?

Kristen shook her head. "All he said was that sometimes he agreed with the group's philosophies about Iraq, and that there might be a big operation going down that would show everyone what this group is capable of. He wants to protect his family's reputation, as I'm sure you can imagine."

Agent Lewis let out a breath, his focus entirely on Kristen. "Okay. Well, that's something to go on, anyway."

"Michael said he'd made sure it looked like I was involved with this, and that I would lose everything if any of this ever came out," Kristen told him, her voice anxious.

"Don't worry about that," he reassured her. "We'd been tracking Mr. Forbes before he even met you. We know you aren't involved." He reached over and flipped on the screen to his computer.

Kristen breathed a sigh of relief at his words. She looked over at Ryan, who just sat there with his arms folded, mirroring her father. Maybe it had been a mistake to let them come in.

"I'm going to show you something," Agent Lewis said. They scooted forward, and he turned the screen so they could all see. "This came through on a Web site feed that is known to broadcast insurgents' tapes. Al-Jazeera is getting set to run it as well, but I thought you might want to see it first."

Their eyes were glued to the small screen, and they squinted to see the image. At first it was fuzzy, but then the static cleared. It was Brandon. He had what looked like a large bruise on the side of his forehead, and his hands were tied and holding a newspaper. He was answering questions, and his eyes kept darting between the camera and the man who was questioning him. "I can't hear what he's saying," Kristen said.

"Yeah, the audio's not so great. Sorry about that. He's mostly giving his name and rank, and the people who have him are saying they're going to prove he's a coward and traitor to his country." The camera focused on a woman beside him who was covered in black. "That's another doctor that was captured with him," the agent explained. Kristen sat back, shocked at what her eyes were seeing. "There's more," Agent Lewis said. After a few minutes, they saw Brandon and the other doctor in a different room; they were apparently operating on someone.

"What's happening?" Kristen asked.

"They're asking him to save the life of Sayed Fahim," the agent said. "If he doesn't save Fahim, he'll be killed himself."

"Sayed Fahim," Kristen breathed. "No." Ryan looked at her, and she saw the grim reality of the situation written on his face. They watched for a few seconds more, and suddenly it looked like something went wrong. Brandon was frantically trying to save the patient. The guards moved in with guns pointed. Then the screen went black. "What happened? Is he okay?" Kristen asked. "Is there any more?"

"That's all there was," Agent Lewis said, his voice full of regret. "I'm sorry."

"Can I see it again?" Kristen asked softly.

He played it back for her, and she gently touched the screen showing Brandon's face. "Thanks for letting us see this privately," Ryan said to the agent.

Kristen's father seemed frozen in place. "Does the military have any rescue mission planned?"

"We don't know anything yet, General," the agent said. "We were wondering if the kidnapping was tied to Mr. Forbes's actions, since Kristen is connected to both, but they seem to be unrelated, a coincidence. Mr. Forbes obviously faces some pretty heavy charges, however."

Kristen stood up. "I don't know if I believe in coincidences, Agent Lewis. I want to talk to Michael. Then I'm going to go back to

Washington, D.C., to use every resource I have to find out what's happening," she said.

"Mr. Forbes is being questioned right now," Agent Lewis informed her.

"I don't care. I just need to ask him one question." Kristen started toward the door. "Can you take me to him?"

"Are you sure you want to do that?" her father asked. "What could you possibly have to say to him?"

"I want to know if he knew about Brandon's kidnapping." She reached for the door. "It's just something I need to do. Then I'll be on the first plane out of here."

"You can't just drop everything and go, Kristy," Ryan told her, following her to the door.

"Watch me," she said calmly. "I need to know what's going on with my brother. Nothing else matters." She reached into her pocket and pulled out her cell phone.

"You know, I have some contacts you could use as well." Ryan said. "We could work together on this. I think Brandon would like that."

At the mention of Brandon's name, Kristen looked up, trying to hold back the tears. Before Ryan could say anything more, though, the general was at their side.

"You're right; we've got to do something. I can use my contacts at the Pentagon to see what the plan is while you're talking to your ex-fiancé."

Kristen took a deep breath. Her father seemed calm enough, his usual matter-of-fact self. She needed to calm down, *but Brandon . . .*

"Brandon can take care of himself," Ryan assured her, seeming to follow her thoughts. "And he's a good doctor—I'm sure he saved Fahim. Let's make a few calls and see what we can find out."

Kristen nodded, biting her lip at Ryan's assessment, and tried to focus on the positives as Ryan was. She followed Agent Lewis. "I'm going to call my boss," she said to Ryan. "Then I'm going to get on the first flight out of here to D.C."

"Okay, when I get back to my office, I'll see what I can find out. As for the trip to Washington—get me a seat next to you and the general." At her look of surprise, he added, "You didn't think I'd let you go alone, did you? I can do more than just make phone calls."

She gave a small smile. "Thanks." They walked down the hall, back the way they had come, stopping in front of a door near the west end of the lobby where Agent Lewis waited.

"Are you sure about this?" the agent asked. Kristen nodded.

Before he could open the door, Ryan held her arm for a moment. "Do you want me to come in with you? I think I should, especially after what happened before with him."

Kristen shook her head. "I'll be fine." Taking a deep breath, she nodded to Agent Lewis, and he opened the door. Michael was sitting in a chair in front of a small table. He looked up when she entered.

"Kristen! I knew you'd come." Kristen just stared at him. It was as if she were looking at a stranger. "Why did you call in the feds? I thought you would at least try to understand." His voice was full of reproach.

Kristen didn't say a word, just sat down in front of him. Agent Lewis stood behind her. "I didn't turn you in. I'm only here to ask you one thing, to get something straight in my head, okay?"

Michael looked at Agent Lewis. "Can we have some privacy?"

"No," Agent Lewis replied unequivocally, then stared off at a point behind Michael's head as if he weren't really listening to their conversation.

Kristen was grateful for the agent's presence, but she was unsure of how willing Michael would be to talk in his presence. "Do you know anything about Brandon's kidnapping?"

"Your brother was kidnapped?" Michael exclaimed, leaning forward. "Who do they think did it?"

Looking at the surprised expression on his face, Kristen wondered if he was telling her the truth. She didn't feel like she knew him anymore at all. Her shoulders sagged.

"They aren't looking at . . . You don't think that I . . ." Michael tipped his head back and let out a breath before facing her again. "Kristen, I wouldn't do that to you. You have to believe me."

Kristen shook her head. "I don't know what to believe anymore, Michael. You've been lying to me for months." She looked him in the eye. "Please, just tell me the truth. They think the kidnappers are part of the organization you were funneling funds to. If you know of any way to contact them, tell me now."

Michael leaned back and folded his arms, his eyes turning hard again. He looked smug, and it angered her. "I do know, Kristen. And I'll tell you if you will use your contacts to help me keep this quiet. Or if the worst happens and it gets out, I want your help spinning this to my advantage. You and Jack are experts at PR. There has to be something you can do for me."

Kristen could only feel rage at his words. She moved around the table so fast that Agent Lewis didn't have time to react. "You owe me this!" she yelled, slapping him. "Tell me what I want to know. This is my brother we're talking about, not a bargaining chip." She pushed the table to the side and bent over him, her face within inches of his. Michael didn't move at all, just watched her in silence.

"This conversation is over," Agent Lewis said as he took Kristen by the arm. She wrenched away and moved back to face her ex-fiancé. "Michael, if you ever loved me at all, please tell me how I can save my brother."

Michael stood, squaring his shoulders and pushing up to his full, six-foot height. He closed his eyes for a moment. "Madj," he said. "And that's all I'll say."

"Your ex-wife? What does she have to do with this? Tell me, Michael."

"I've told you too much already, Kristen. But I did love you. I want you to know that." He looked down at her and reached out to touch her face. She flinched and backed away.

"Tell me how to contact this group," she pleaded, feeling tears welling in her eyes.

Michael shook his head, his hand falling to his side. "I've done all I can do. Trust me. And believe me when I say I loved you."

The tears rolled silently down her cheeks. Straightening her shoulders, she smoothed her blouse and raised her chin. "Good-bye, Michael."

She strode past Agent Lewis, wiping her tears away and regaining her composure before she opened the door. Ryan was right outside. Kristen straightened her back and tried not to appear upset.

"Are you okay?" he asked.

She nodded, her lips set in a grim line. "I need to get out of here." She blew out a breath and set her shoulders. Both Ryan and her father flanked her as they walked toward the entrance, each lost in their own thoughts. Kristen's phone rang, and she absently picked it up as they walked. "Kristen Shepherd."

Kristen slowed her pace, and so did the men beside her when they saw the large contingent of press corps gathered near the front doors of the auditorium. "What the devil?" Ryan said. "Oh no." He turned back toward Kristen, a stricken look on his face. She gave the person on the other end of the line a "no comment" and quickly clapped her phone shut.

"Story's out, apparently," she said curtly. "Now what should we do?"

CHAPTER 10

Kristen was grateful that Ryan and her father were there to hold the press at bay while she pushed through to her car. The general shouted that he'd meet up with her later, and she nodded as he ran off to get to his car. Everyone was yelling questions, wanting a reaction to Michael's arrest and Brandon's capture, but she wasn't ready to respond. *I can't believe they got hold of the story so quickly!* But she knew news and rumor traveled fast in journalism circles, especially with the Internet. Usually, though, she was the one putting out the story—not the focus of it. Taking a deep breath, she tried to calm her pounding heart. Ryan helped her into the car and shut the door, repeating "no comment" several times before he got in himself. They backed up slowly, not wanting to hurt anyone, and as soon as they were clear, they sped down the street.

"Where are we going?"

"I thought my office might be a good place to go right now. There's security, phones, and a computer."

She nodded. "Thanks, Ryan." She turned on the radio and began flipping channels. "I wonder if there's any news about the debate yet."

She couldn't find anything, so she sat back, trying to process everything that had happened in the last hour and wondering where she should go from here. She knew she could count on Senator Reed to give her information since he oversaw several National Defense Committees. They'd gotten to know each other well when she'd run his campaign. She ran down other lists of contacts, mentally discarding and prioritizing who she would call first. By the time they reached the state government building, she was ready.

They walked down the mostly deserted hall to Ryan's office. Kristen assumed all but a few workers were at the debates, and she wondered how everything was going. When Ryan opened the door and turned on the lights, he invited her to sit down while he booted up his computer.

"This is nice." She leaned down and looked at a family picture he had displayed. "That's how I remember your family," she said. "You always seemed happy."

His face clouded over. "We had our hard times, too."

"I know, but you were always the family I wanted to have." She sat back down.

"You were practically family anyway, with as much time as we all spent together." He turned on the small television and flipped through the channels. Several stations were carrying the breaking news of Michael's arrest and Brandon's capture, showing Brandon's wounded face on-screen then cutting to Michael's final words to Kristen—"If I go down, you go down." Speculation was running rampant. Kristen sighed and turned away from the television but snapped her attention back to the screen when she heard Brandon's voice. ". . . Brandon Shepherd, I'm a doctor at the field hospital in al-Qaim and a captain in the United States Army." Kristen watched silently as the image of Brandon's face was replaced with the anchor's, and the news went on to the next story. She looked away. Ryan clicked it off.

"Okay, what do you want to do first?" he asked her.

She listed off the names she'd thought of in the car. Ryan looked impressed. She couldn't stop to analyze how that made her feel, but she hadn't been trying to impress him. "I'll start there and work my way down," she told him. Her phone rang and, when she answered, she kept it short and hung up quickly.

"What did your dad say?" Ryan asked, shuffling some papers on his desk.

"How did you know it was my dad?" Kristen asked, turning toward him in surprise.

"From your tone of voice. And the fact that it was short and sweet," Ryan said, glancing at her with a chuckle.

Kristen sighed ruefully and slipped her phone back into her pocket. "I'll give you that. My father is not a man of many words. I guess I'm the same way with him." She paced a little and began chewing on the end of her thumbnail.

"Some things never change," Ryan said with a grin. "You always chewed on your nails when you had something on your mind. So tell me, what did your dad say?"

Kristen immediately put her hand at her side, rubbing her fingers together. "I've worked really hard at breaking that habit, you know. But today is just a little overwhelming." She resumed her pacing. "Like we discussed, my dad is working the military angle, and I'm working the political. That way, we should get some corroborating evidence. We're all on the same flight to Washington." She looked at her watch. "We'll need to be at the airport in a few hours."

Ryan looked surprised. "Your dad got us a flight that fast?"

She smiled. "I told you we have connections. Sometimes having a dad who practically called the Pentagon home is a plus."

They got to work, Ryan calling some government officials he knew and Kristen working her end. After about half an hour, she hung up and ran her hands through her hair. Ryan quickly wrapped up his call. "What did you find out?"

"Nothing much," she replied grimly. "He was picking up some wounded soldiers in the field when they were attacked. The soldiers they were treating, the pilot, and the crew member were all found dead. It's a miracle Brandon even made it out alive. The female doctor with him is named Rachel Fielding. That's all I've gotten so far."

"Has anyone talked about a rescue mission?"

"Not yet. I'm getting stonewalled on that. Maybe when I talk with someone face-to-face in Washington, I'll get somewhere." She massaged her neck. "I can't even imagine what he's going through right now."

Ryan came and stood in front of her, catching her eye. He'd taken off his jacket and rolled up his sleeves, and with his hair mussed, he looked more boyish, like the Ryan she'd known and once loved. It made her heart skip a beat. He finally spoke. "Well, we'll both be praying for him, and I'm sure he'll feel that," he said. Kristen blinked at his words, then turned her face away.

"I know Brandon joined a church right before he was deployed, but I haven't prayed for anything in a very long time, Ryan," Kristen admitted, the worry evident in her voice. She reluctantly raised her eyes to look at him. "There never seemed to be any point, and I seemed to be doing okay on my own. Would God even listen to me now?" The feeling in the room seemed to change with her statement, and Ryan moved closer to her. Kristen closed her eyes, breathing in his aftershave and feeling strangely comforted by its familiar scent.

The mood was broken, however, when the intercom buzzed. He stepped away and looked at her for a moment, his gaze locking with hers before he strode over to pick up the call. He leaned on the desk, phone in hand, and listened intently for a moment. "Okay," he said into the receiver, then gave a long pause. "You've got to be kidding."

His tone was incredulous, and Kristen turned to look at him. "What is it?"

He hung up the phone, shaking his head. "That was a heads-up. Apparently calls have been made by some pretty reputable journalists. Favors have been called in, and people have drawn some rough connections." He looked at her as if he didn't want to say anything else but knew he had to. "Connections that aren't true. The top news story will be how you've been using funds to support a terrorist organization—and now the deal went bad, and Brandon's kidnapping is intended to force your hand. They're saying that anonymous sources have confirmed that the terrorists have turned on you and are using your brother as leverage."

"What?" Kristen sat down, her knees no longer able to hold her. Who were the anonymous sources? Was Michael or his family part of this—was this a ploy to deflect the blame from him? Should she issue a statement? Her stomach clenched in anger. Why would they report it like this? Her shoulders sagged when she realized that she'd used the press in much the same way herself. It was all spin to create a story that would bring in ratings. And who was she fooling? It *was* incredible that her fiancé and her brother were both possibly linked to the same group. If it was the case, she was the common link between the two, and it made for a sensational story.

The only lead she had was Michael's ex-wife. Kristen made a mental note to find out everything she could about Madj Forbes and where her last known location was. She hoped against hope that Madj would know of a way to contact this group and get her brother and herself out of this mess. She ran her hands through her hair again, trying to collect her thoughts. She needed to think clearly, but she was having a hard time focusing. Leaning forward, her elbows on her knees, she put her hand to her forehead.

Ryan stood in front of her and, from the look on his face, he had something to say. "Is there anything you want to tell me?" he asked, his voice solemn.

"What do you mean?" she asked, looking up at him, furrowing her brow and tilting her head to the side to rub her neck.

"Is there any truth to it? Were you involved in this at all?" He leaned against the arm of the couch, watching her carefully. "I mean, I know what you told the agent. I just want to know the real story."

Kristen went rigid; she immediately dropped her hands to her sides and stood, her eyes flashing angrily. "What I told the agent was the truth, Ryan. I am not a liar." She started to gather her things. "Why did I let myself believe that anything had changed? I should have known that I still couldn't count on you," she mumbled to herself. Kristen marched to the door, but he quickly caught up to her.

"Kristy, I'm sorry. Please don't go. You don't understand." She turned on him so fast he stepped back in surprise.

"You bet I don't understand! There was a time that you knew me better than that."

Ryan took her arm, his green eyes filled with regret. "I'm sorry."

"What changed?" she challenged, shaking her head and refusing to hear his apology. "I'd really like to know what changed you."

Ryan sighed and took his hand off her arm. "My wife."

Kristen stepped back toward him, ready for battle, then stopped herself as the words he'd spoken set in. Instead, she slowly folded her arms and stood directly in front of him. "What do you mean?" she asked, her voice steadier.

He stared at her for a moment, as if he were debating whether to tell her. He took a deep breath and spoke quickly. "She hid a very serious gambling addiction from me. I only found out about it after she'd maxed out my credit cards and ruined us financially. Everything I'd thought was real had been a lie. And it destroyed us." He looked away, then walked back to his desk and sat down, leaning his arms on the shiny wood surface. "It changed me, Kristy. It made me take a look at who I am. Sometimes I'm overly suspicious now when things seem too coincidental. I lived an illusion so long that I don't trust my instincts anymore."

Kristen stood still, her heart full of understanding. "Obviously you know that I'm dealing with trust issues because of someone I loved, too. Looks like we've both been burned." She walked back to the couch, sinking down into its cushions. "I really am sorry, Ryan. I know what it feels like to have the rug pulled out from under you and to be made to feel the fool."

He nodded. "I know my divorce happened a long time ago, but the scars have been slow in healing." He shifted in the leather chair and leaned over the desk on his elbows. "Well, I've been burned once, but you've been burned twice that I know of. And I'm sorry to say I was one of the people who hurt you." He raised his eyes to meet hers.

Kristen shook her head. "That doesn't hurt now. When you shared things I never thought you'd tell another soul . . . well, I felt like you'd thrown away something that had been wonderful between us. You'd always been my safe place, and all of the sudden you weren't safe anymore." Tipping her head, she gave him a small smile. "I know now that you didn't mean to hurt me that way, and I realize you didn't know how important all that was to me. I really am sorry for the way I've thought of you since that night."

"That bad, huh? he asked, wrinkling his nose.

"Yeah, pretty bad," she said, smiling at him.

"I'd suggest we start over, but I don't want to do that," he said. "I want you to know without having to test the waters again—that you can trust me. With anything." His voice was earnest, and she felt like a teenager all over again, the slow burn creeping up her face and the flutter starting in her stomach. It scared her a little to have those feelings come back so quickly. Just a short time ago, she'd thought they'd been buried forever.

Standing back up, she knew it was time to go. "Thank you. I'd better go home and pack."

He stood and came around the desk, stopping in front of her. With the desk crowding them, there were mere inches between them. He was close—too close—and Kristen's breath caught in her throat. All of the sudden it felt like there was electricity in the air, causing Kristen's nerve endings to hum with the tension. Ryan seemed to be waiting for her to say something, but she didn't know what to say. They had both been through a lot, had both changed. Yet Kristen realized in that moment that her feelings toward him had remained the same. But what she didn't know was how he really felt about her.

Ryan thrust his hands into his pockets. "Kristy, I . . ."

Before he could say anything else, there was a knock at the door followed by the general striding through it. "What's going on here? Why aren't you on your way to the airport?" he said, his voice bellowing through the room. "We don't have time to waste."

Kristen would have laughed if it wouldn't have looked like she was losing it; her father's timing was impeccable as always.

"We're on our way, sir. Were you able to find out anything about Brandon?" Ryan asked.

"Of course. We're meeting at the Pentagon tomorrow morning. Are things settled here?"

He looked at Kristen, and she knew he fully expected her to say yes.

"Of course they are, sir. Let's go," she said, turning to gather up her things and catch her breath from what had just happened with Ryan.

Ryan held his hand at her back as she followed her father to the door, and the warmth from it traveled all the way through her. "Are you okay?" he asked her softly enough that only she could hear.

So many thoughts were running through her head in different directions that she was having a hard time gathering them. What had Ryan been about to say? Could she really trust him? Mentally shaking herself, she tried to focus on her brother. "I have to be okay. Brandon needs me," was all she said. She thought of his face on the video and silently vowed she would find him— no matter what.

CHAPTER 11

Kristen called Ryan's room, hoping to find him there. She massaged her temples and knew she needed to sleep soon, but she felt like she was running out of time. They had gotten into Washington late and had spent most of the night and all of the following morning trying to contact anyone who might know anything about Brandon's whereabouts. Rolling her shoulders, she waited while the phone in Ryan's room rang again. Kristen willed him to pick up, since she really wanted him in on this meeting. She audibly sighed with relief when he finally answered. "Ryan, it's Kristen. My dad got ahold of one of his old army buddies who's agreed to meet us here at Bistro Bis downstairs in the hotel. Can you come down? He says he has some information for us."

When she was sure Ryan was on his way, she hung up. He sounded tired, and she knew he'd been on the phone half the night trying to tie up some loose ends with the governor. It had been a terrible time for him to leave. She'd tried to convince him to go back, but he wouldn't hear of it. He'd emphatically stated that he wanted to be with her, and she believed him. As she slowly walked to the restaurant, her cell phone rang. "Hello?"

"Is this Kristen Shepherd?" a heavily accented female voice asked.

"Yes, who is this?"

"Never mind who I am. Just tell me where Michael is."

Kristen almost dropped her phone, her senses immediately on alert. "Is this Madj?" There was no answer, so Kristen continued. "He's been taken in for questioning. I'm not sure where. Do you know where my brother is? Can you help me find him or contact the people who have him?" She lowered her voice, realizing she was standing in a very public place.

There was silence on the other end of the line, and Kristen wondered if the woman had hung up. But then the voice said, "Find out where Michael is being held; I will contact you when you get to al-Qaim."

"How did you know I'm coming . . ." Kristen started to say, then stopped herself. Were her phone calls being monitored somehow? She decided she didn't want to know. "Where will I meet you?"

"I will find you. Don't tell anyone about this call or there will be consequences."

"Please," Kristen began, but the call had already been disconnected. She slowly closed the phone. Could Madj help her? Was it just a ploy? Her mind raced with possibilities. Should she call Agent Lewis or tell her father? Madj had warned her. Would Brandon suffer if she told anyone?

Just then Kristen felt hands on her shoulders, and she jumped in surprise.

"Sorry, I didn't mean to startle you," Ryan said, backing up. "You seemed lost in thought. Who was that?"

Kristen bit her lip. She needed to protect Brandon, but was giving in to terrorist demands a good idea?

"Tell me." Ryan said. "From the look on your face, it was pretty important. Was it about Brandon?"

She looked into his face, so sincere, and thought of the things he'd shared with her about his ex-wife. She knew they'd both learned from their mistakes and that she could trust him to protect Brandon by not doing anything stupid. She took a breath and drew him into a small corner, pulling him very close so that no one else could overhear their conversation. "I think it was Michael's ex-wife, Madj. She said if I find out where they've taken Michael for her, she'll tell me how to contact Brandon." Tilting her head, she put her hand on his chest and met his eyes. "She said if I told anyone there would be consequences. I think we need to keep this between us for now."

He watched her for a moment, his gaze searching her face. "I promise."

She smiled, aware of a new dynamic between them; it was as if a previously blocked path had opened. Her heart felt lighter, and she reached down and squeezed his hand. They turned to walk into the restaurant, and he didn't drop her hand, even when they came into view of the general. The gesture made Kristen's heart jump. Her father didn't seem to notice, but when Kristen saw that he was standing near the front of the restaurant waiting for them, she instinctively quickened her step. Her father did not like to be kept waiting. Ryan seemed to understand, and he lengthened his stride to keep up.

Before she could go any farther, however, a tall, wiry man wearing an apron approached her, waving his arms in the air. "I never thought I'd see you again," he said to Kristen, his voice thick with a French accent. "You have graced us with your presence, mon chérie," he said as he reached for her hand and kissed the back of it.

"Jacques, I've missed you," she said, smiling at his greeting. Jacques never did anything halfway. "No one can cook grilled salmon like you."

He kissed the tips of his fingers. "Yes, you have a weak spot for my fish. *C'est magnifique, n'est-ce pas?*"

She laughed. *"Oui, c'est magnifique.* You know I can't resist the oysters either."

He leaned closer. "They say oysters are the food of love, you know."

"I don't have any time for love," she assured him.

"That's too bad," he said as he winked at her. "You're much too beautiful to be too busy for love."

"I'm glad you made it," the general said to Ryan.

Kristen's smile died at the reminder of why they were there, but she quickly pasted another one on. "Jacques, this is my father, General Grant Shepherd, and this is my friend Ryan Jameson."

The little glint in Jacques's eyes grew bigger as he vigorously shook Ryan's hand. "Ah, a friend? Does he not see how beautiful you are?" he said over his shoulder to Kristen.

She rolled her eyes. "Jacques, stop. Don't embarrass me."

Ryan merely grinned and said, "Of course." Jacques gave Kristen another wink at Ryan's answer and shook her father's hand before turning back to her.

"We need a table for four today, my friend. Do you have anything available?" Kristen asked.

"For you, mon chérie, I always have a table. Come and see me before you leave, though, *d'accord?*" She nodded, and he kissed her on both cheeks. "It is good to see you again."

"Say hello to Sylvie for me," she said as they moved to their table. He waved back at her. They passed the bar area, which was loud, even though it wasn't really crowded. There was a balcony above them, and the main dining room featured tables where diners could watch Jacques and his staff working in the glass-fronted kitchen, but Kristen was led by a hostess to a dining table in a corner with a discreet translucent screen, making it feel very private.

She sat down and smiled at Ryan and her father. "It feels like coming home," she said. "I used to spend a lot of time here when I was working with Senator Reed." She looked at Ryan. "Jacques's grilled salmon is incredible. The red snapper is good, too, if you're really hungry."

"Do they have any good steak?" her father asked. "You know I don't like fish."

"The steak is so tender it'll melt in your mouth." After a few moments, they ordered, and Kristen turned as the hostess brought a uniformed man to their table. Her father rose, and the two men shook hands.

"Clayton, it's good to see you. Thanks for meeting us here," the general said, slapping the man on the back. Ryan slid over next to Kristen while the general sat across from them.

"I can't stay long, but I felt I owed this to you, Grant. I know you must be very concerned about your son." Clayton looked over at Kristen. "I don't think we've met before."

"Sorry, Clayton, this is my daughter, Kristen, and a friend of the family, Ryan Jameson." Clayton reached out and shook their hands. "Kristen, Ryan, this is one of my oldest friends, General Clayton Ashling." The general turned back to his friend. "What do you know about Brandon?"

Clayton leaned forward. "This is strictly off the record, mind you. That's why I didn't want to talk about it at the Pentagon. Too many ears. But I'm doing this because you're an old friend of mine." He stopped while the waitress set out their drinks.

"Would you like something, Clay?" General Shepherd asked.

"No, I can't stay long," he said. "I'm expected back. They're trying to pinpoint the location on your son, but some of the military are hesitating because of what was on that video."

"What do you mean?" the general asked, keeping his voice even.

"Well, at the end of the video it looked like . . ." He lowered his eyes. "It looked like the operation may have gone bad," he said, his meaning clear.

"So they don't know if he's still alive, and if he is alive, whether he's even worth rescuing. Is that what you're telling me?" the general said, his voice rising. "My son is serving his country."

"I know that, Grant," Clayton said. "I'm just telling you what's going on."

"I appreciate that," General Shepherd said, lowering his voice. "Tell me what information they have."

"They have his last known location as well as some intel on a local that was working on his base as an interpreter. He disappeared soon after Brandon and Dr. Fielding were kidnapped, and they think there's a connection there. They're following up on the lead." Clayton got up. "That's all I know, Grant. I'm sorry. If anything else comes up, I'll let you know."

When the waitress brought their meals, the group ate in silence, lost in their own thoughts. "What are we going to do, Dad?" Kristen asked. "They're not going to let us in on anything, and it doesn't seem like everyone is on board with the rescue." She sighed. "I was stonewalled everywhere I went this morning, like there's a gag order on this thing or something."

"Me too," Ryan chimed in. "The governor even made a few calls for me, but neither of us got anywhere."

Kristen dabbed at her lips with her napkin before turning surprised eyes to Ryan. "The governor made calls for us?"

"Well, Brandon is a Massachusetts soldier." Ryan ran his hand through his hair. "And besides, the governor's a really nice guy."

"Did he say how the debate turned out last night?" she asked, her mouth turning up in a grin. "Did he call you because he needed a sympathetic ear?"

"The governor said he felt really good about the debate, thank you very much. How about you? Was Mr. Addison making any phone calls to you looking for a sympathetic ear?" Ryan sipped his drink, watching her.

She shrugged her shoulders. "I'm off the campaign, so he wouldn't be calling me. My boss, Jack Pierson, took over last I heard."

Ryan almost choked. "Jack Pierson took over? *The* Jack Pierson?"

"Yeah, *the* Jack Pierson. I guess his reputation precedes him." Kristen smirked at Ryan's reaction.

Ryan tried to cover his surprise, but Kristen read him easily and stifled a chuckle. "Have you talked to Agent Lewis at all?" he asked, conspicuously changing the subject. "Do you have any idea what's happening with Michael? The press is going nuts with this story. You would think Lewis would help you out."

His words wiped the smile off of her face, reminding her of what was at stake. "I haven't talked to him, and I'm sure he thinks I can handle something like this on my own." She shifted uncomfortably and glanced at her father, thinking of her conversation with Madj. "Agent Lewis has all my numbers, and he gave me his in case I did need anything. But what can he do, really? I think that my main focus, beyond getting any information I can about Brandon, has to be helping Jack make sure that Mr. Addison's campaign doesn't suffer. The press is blowing everything out of proportion, and I don't want that to hurt Mr. Addison's chances."

"You're doing damage control," Ryan said, taking a sip of water. "The Top is spinning fast and strong."

"It's all under control, rest assured," Kristen said with confidence, enjoying the back-and-forth banter. She held back a smile and placed her fork and knife together on her plate before finishing her mineral water. "I need to go back to the hotel and get some sleep. I'm exhausted." She turned to her father. "What about you, Dad?"

The general had been silent up to this point, but he took a deep breath and looked closely at Kristen. "I'm going to make arrangements to be on the next military flight to Iraq, Kristen." He said it slowly, as if he wanted her to understand so he wouldn't have to repeat himself. "I need to be over there, pressuring the right people to search for Brandon."

"Okay, I'm going with you," she said firmly, all thoughts of sleep gone.

"No, it's too dangerous," the general shot back immediately. "I don't want to have to worry about both you and your brother."

"I've been on my own a long time," she said, her resentment creeping into her voice. "Besides, when have you ever worried about me?"

The general pursed his lips until they were an angry white line. "You will not speak to me that way, young lady."

Kristen looked at her father's face and saw the same worry and concern she was feeling. Her shoulders sagged. "I'm sorry. I'm just tired and anxious about Brandon. Please, I need to go with you. We can do this together. I can help you—I know some Arabic, remember?" She was pleading, and her eyes were starting to water, but to her credit, she held them in check. Kristen knew he would see tears as a sign of weakness, and then she'd never be allowed to go.

The general looked thoughtful for a moment. "Okay, I'll see what I can do about getting us some seats to Iraq. It won't be first class, though. You know that. Probably something military."

Kristen nodded, the relief in her voice evident. "Thank you."

Ryan watched them both, his expression serious. "I'd like to come along as well, General."

"Splendid idea," he said as he motioned to the waiter for the check. "Then you can watch Kristen while I work."

Kristen's felt her jaw tighten at her father's last comment. She held her tongue this time—at least she was going. She picked up her purse and slid out from the table. "I'll go freshen up then and maybe rest a while. Call me when we're ready to go." She thought about heading back to her Washington apartment to pick up a few things, but with her father's attitude, she knew that he might just leave without her while she was gone. The suitcase she'd brought with her would have to do.

Ryan wiped his mouth on his napkin and stood with her. She swayed slightly toward him, and he took her arm. "Are you okay?"

"I'm fine," she said absently. "Thanks, Ryan." She started toward the door, asking their hostess to tell Jacques she was leaving. Before she had passed the bar, Jacques was at her side. "My compliments to the chef," she said warmly. "You've outdone yourself this time."

Jacques smiled at the praise. "Merci," he said. "You are leaving so soon? You are always on the go. You need to slow down, mon chérie."

Kristen glanced back at Ryan, who was watching her with a bemused look on his face. "I will, Jacques. Just for you."

He kissed both her cheeks. "Come back soon," he said. "I will save your table for you."

She squeezed his hands. "Thank you, old friend." She turned to the door before anyone could see the tears brimming in her eyes. She needed to be alone and curl up on her bed to have a good cry. Hurrying past the rich cherry furnishings, her shoes clicked on the tile as she walked to the lobby. She pushed the button on the elevator and willed it to come quickly. It didn't come quickly enough, as her father and Ryan caught up with her. "What's the hurry, Kristy?" Ryan asked.

"I'm just tired," she said, trying to keep her voice even, "and worried about my brother."

He took her arm and turned her around to look at him. "I'm as worried about Brandon as you are, but I'm also concerned about you. You're under a lot of strain."

One part of her wanted nothing more than to collapse into his arms and cry out her fear and frustration, but with *the general* looking on, that was impossible. She had to be strong. "Thanks, Ryan. I'm sure I'll feel better after a shower and a little rest."

The threesome climbed onto the elevator and were soon walking down the hall to their respective rooms. "I'll call you as soon as the arrangements are made," her father said, stopping first at his room. He disappeared inside, leaving Kristen and Ryan to walk a little farther down the hall. Ryan stopped in front of Kristen's door.

"Are you sure you're going to be all right?" he asked, moving closer to her and putting his hands on her shoulders.

A slow heat moved from Kristen's shoulders to her face. The electricity was back. His touch seemed to ignite something in her, a lingering burn that permeated her entire body. She wanted to be near him, needed to be held by him if only for just a moment. Her mind seemed to be moving in slow motion as she leaned forward and slid her arms around Ryan's neck, hugging him close. His arms slipped around her waist, and he pulled her more tightly to him. She truly felt like she belonged there, like the defenses she had built up were slowly being peeled away. She stayed in the embrace for a moment longer, then pulled back. "I . . ."

"Kristy," Ryan said, covering her mouth with his finger to quiet her. "I know this is a stressful situation and feelings might be heightened, but I want you to know that I've always cared about you. Maybe it wasn't the right time for us before, but . . ." The word hung in the air.

The green eyes she'd dreamed of as a girl were looking at her now in the way she had wished he would looked at her then. It was a lot to take in. Part of her wanted to tell him her feelings had never changed, but the rest of her mind argued that he hadn't thought of her as anything more than a kid sister before. She shook her head. "I'm so tired, Ryan. I'm sorry."

She hated seeing the disappointed look on his face, but he stepped back. "Just think about it, okay?" he asked. His voice became deeper. "You trusted me with your heart once. I'd like a second chance. I just wanted you to know that. You don't have to say anything right now."

She nodded and squeezed his hand before she let herself into her room. Leaning against the door, she brought a hand to her stomach and until the fluttering subsided. "After all these years," she whispered to herself. Then, still smiling, she laid down on the bed and relived the moment.

CHAPTER 12

The adrenaline rushing through Kristen's veins kept her awake through most of the layovers on the way to Iraq. She had tried to find out from Agent Lewis what had happened to Michael, but he had refused to give her any information, only saying that Michael was still being questioned. He had quizzed her on why she wanted to know, asking if she'd been contacted by anyone who was connected to Michael, but Kristen had successfully dodged the questions, saying that he had been her fiancé, so of course she would be interested. She had practically begged him for something, any tidbit of information, but he had been adamant. It was frustrating, and Kristen didn't know what she would tell Madj—or if anything she had to say would, in fact, help her brother.

Kristen racked her brain for any detail she could remember about Madj. She knew Madj and Michael had been married for a little over five years and that they'd met while he was serving as a diplomatic aide in Saudi Arabia. She'd seen a picture of Madj once, smiling into the camera with large brown eyes and a pretty smile. Kristen wished now that she had asked Michael more about why their marriage hadn't lasted, but hindsight was 20/20. He never really seemed to want to talk about her, and Kristen hadn't wanted to bring up painful memories, so she'd let it go. His reticence made more sense to her now, though, and she realized that not finding out more about his failed marriage hadn't been the smartest move.

Settling back in her seat, she looked around the 747 military aircraft that was taking them to Kuwait. She was surrounded by soldiers in camouflage with M-16s and 9mm pistols. The soldiers joked around and laughed with each other, looking curiously at Kristen, Ryan, and the general, but no one approached them. She felt conspicuous but was so tired she eventually fell asleep as they'd headed out over the Atlantic. She got out to stretch her legs for a short layover in Germany, then watched as they flew into the Kuwaiti International Airport.

Some of the soldiers had, by this time, found out that Kristen and her father were the family of the kidnapped doctor, and several had offered their condolences, stating unequivocally that Brandon would be found. It brought Kristen to tears, seeing their earnestness.

They taxied onto the runway in Kuwait, and the stairs were lowered. An air of excitement permeated the cabin, and everything seemed to start moving in fast motion. It was dark and not quite as hot as Kristen had imagined. The ground crew was unloading the gear as the soldiers were escorted to a dirt field, carrying their weapons and bags. Kristen was curious about where the soldiers were going and followed behind at a discreet distance. Ryan easily caught up to her.

"Where are you going?" he asked. "We better stay near your father."

Kristen nodded. "I wanted to see what they were going to do," she said as she pointed to the soldiers now huddled together in small groups on the dirt lot.

As she spoke, several buses rolled up. "Wouldn't they be good terrorist targets in those buses so obviously coming from the airport?" Kristen said, thinking aloud.

"They'll be given security rounds," her father said from behind her. "The weapons they have now don't have any ammunition in them, but that will be taken care of on the bus." He glanced over at the soldiers. "They'll be prepared if they're ambushed. Our car is waiting, and I have our itinerary. We'll be heading to the nearest U.S. base in Kuwait, and from there, we'll fly to Iraq. We have to go." He turned around and walked back the way he'd come, expecting Ryan and Kristen to follow.

They drove for half an hour before reaching the military base. After being offered "mid-rats," which Kristen learned was army lingo for midnight meal, their ID cards were scanned into a huge computer that kept track of all U.S. military personnel in that "theater." After a short security briefing, the general, Kristen, and Ryan were taken to a resting area so they could freshen up since their flight didn't leave until later that night. The captain explained that their stick—their *flight,* he clarified—would be with a mixed squadron. This meant that if one of the planes were to go down, they wouldn't lose all their mechanics or any full group of specialists. They traveled at night with the lights off to avoid being attacked by rockets.

Kristen felt slightly wary, but if it meant moving closer to her brother, she was all for it. She felt completely worn out, physically and emotionally, and she desperately wished for a shower, a change of clothes, and her soft bed at home. But all that was secondary to finding Brandon, and she knew time was running out. Ryan put his arm around her, and she looked at him gratefully. She was so glad he'd come. It made it a little more bearable to have his support. Her thoughts flitted back to the embrace they'd shared, and her insides melted at the memory. Stealing a glance at him, she returned his smile, thinking about how easily she'd fallen back into his orbit, drawn in by the kind of man that he was. Knowing it was not the right moment for such thoughts, she tried to concentrate on the information they were being given before being flown into Iraq.

Her father asked several questions about what they should expect in al-Qaim, and Kristen was surprised at how comfortable and relaxed he seemed in these militaristic surroundings. It was like he was a different person. He was definitely in his element, and it was a side of him she hadn't seen. Turning her head away from the sight of Ryan and her father, she wondered if perhaps she'd been too hard on her dad, judging him by only part of the picture. Too tired to think, she reminded herself to deal with one thing at a time.

* * *

As night fell, they were jammed into a C-130 with a squadron of soldiers. It was hot and stuffy with all the gear, and the plane flew erratically to avoid becoming a target, making some soldiers sick. The general dozed through most of it, but Kristen was wide awake. Ryan moved closer to her and took her hand, running lazy circles over her palm with his thumb. His touch sent shivers up and down her spine, and she bit her lip.

"How are you holding up?" he asked, tilting his head to meet her eyes.

She turned away from him, not wanting him to notice her tears. He gently turned her face back to his. "What's wrong?"

Her brow furrowed. "Oh, Ryan, what if we're too late?"

"Don't think like that. Brandon's going to be rescued." She swiped at the tears that trickled down her cheeks, and he put his arm around her. "Don't give up hope, Kristen."

Sighing, she shook her head. "I'm trying, Ryan. I keep thinking I'll feel something in here," she tapped her chest, "if Brandon is really gone."

He tightened his arm around her. "Then he's not gone. Hold onto that."

She nodded but didn't say anything else. It felt so good to be able to share her thoughts and fears with someone. Momentarily pushing all of her worries aside, Kristen tried to focus on the reason they had come to Iraq. "I'm glad you're here," she said finally.

Ryan drew her snugly into the crook of his arm. "Me too."

When they landed it was still dark. While they were rolling on the runway, the back of the plane was opened, and a large load of cargo dropped out. When that was complete, everyone filed off and was loaded into trucks to rejoin their respective squadron. Army personnel greeted the threesome and escorted them to their convoy. "You'll be on your way to al-Qaim in a few minutes, sir," one man said, saluting Kristen's father. The general saluted back, then climbed up in front.

"The sooner the better," Kristen's father muttered.

Kristen couldn't believe how hot it was even at night. Pulling her shirt collar away from her body, she winced. After traveling as much as she had in the last two days, she was ready for a change of clothes. But that would have to wait because the trucks were beginning to move out. Ryan climbed in beside her, and she leaned against his shoulder. "I'm so tired," she murmured, "but I don't think I could sleep a wink." He stroked her hair, much like her mother had done when she was a little girl. Within moments she was asleep.

* * *

Kristen awoke feeling disoriented. She was still hot, and a rhythmic rocking she felt told her she was still in the truck. Ryan was dozing beside her. She watched him sleep, his features peaceful. His dark hair curled slightly against his shirt collar, and his chin was stubbly since he hadn't shaved in almost two days. She reached up to feel it, running the back of her hand down his jawline. Eyes still closed, he reached out and gently grabbed her fingers before she could pull away, making her cheeks flush. "Good morning," he said, sitting taller and leaning toward her. "Did you get much sleep?"

"A little," she admitted. "I'm not usually able to sleep in moving vehicles, but I guess I was pretty tired."

He smiled. "You needed some rest so you would be ready for today."

She nodded as the trucks rolled to a stop. "Here we are," the general said over his shoulder. The convoy rolled slightly forward, and the general got out to be greeted by the commanding officer. "I'm Colonel Palmer," he said. "You must be General Shepherd."

"I am." He nodded. "Has there been any news about my son?"

The colonel lifted his arm toward the buildings behind him. "Let's talk in my office." He led them to the hospital and down a corridor to a small but well-kept room. When they were all inside, he sat down behind a small desk and motioned for them to sit in some folding chairs. "First of all, I want you to know that Captain Shepherd is a fine doctor and a fine man. I have enjoyed working with him. The other doctor that he's with, Dr. Rachel Fielding, is a fine person as well. We are doing everything we can to find them and bring them back safely. However, we're getting some mixed signals from Washington."

"Thank you for your efforts," Kristen said. "I hope you're not letting Washington's attitude hinder you. Has there been anything new?"

The colonel looked over some papers on his desk, then turned his attention back to them. "This is what we know so far. The group that claims to have them is making contact through the Mujahedeen Shura Council, which is an umbrella organization for the insurgent factions in Iraq. They've broadcast the video I'm sure you've seen over the Internet, but we can't authenticate it, and we have no other proof—no dog tags, ID cards, or anything else—beyond that initial video."

"Why would you need something other than the video?" the general asked. "Do you think it's been fabricated?"

"No, but the Pentagon's official statement is that they don't have an independent confirmation that any of our military personnel is being held, and that they won't take action until they do," the colonel answered. "It does help that the video of both doctors was broadcast on a Web site known for publishing messages from insurgent groups in Iraq, however, and Captain Shepherd is holding a dated newspaper that matches with the day he disappeared."

The colonel stood and leaned over a desk that had a map on it. "This is what we've done so far, sir." He pointed to several locations on the map. "We've deployed fighter jets, helicopters, and unmanned drones to help us find them. We think they were traveling in this area, toward Fallujah, so that's where we started searching first." He sat back down. "We've got a curfew in the area, and we've been doing some house-to-house raids on suspected informants, but so far we haven't come up with anything."

"What about this interpreter that may have helped the kidnappers?" General Shepherd asked.

"He worked here occasionally. When we questioned his wife, she said that two of her sons had been kidnapped and that her husband had been forced to help the insurgents capture a doctor in exchange for the boys' freedom. When Dr. Fielding went on a dust-off to evacuate two critically wounded soldiers, Dr. Shepherd went with her; the helicopter was ambushed and then lost in a sandstorm. The only thing we can figure is that Nazir must have overheard the approximate location of where the medics would be and passed the information along. The sandstorm hit during the evacuation and . . . well . . . it was a matter of being in the wrong place at the wrong time."

The colonel seemed so matter-of-fact. Kristen grasped the arms of her chair. "Did the interpreter's wife say anything else that might help us find out where Brandon is?"

"She was pretty shaken up," Colonel Palmer said, shaking his head.

"I want to talk to her," Kristen told him. "Maybe she's remembered something that might help Brandon."

"I don't think that's a good idea, but I'll consider it," he said kindly. He stood, and everyone stood with him. "The Iraqi foreign minister won't confirm anything or utter the word *kidnapped,* but he did say that he hoped both doctors would be found as soon as possible." Colonel Palmer opened the door. "So if we're going to find them, we're going to have to do it on our own."

He led them back down the hall and out onto the base. "Kidnappings of U.S. service members are actually quite rare," he told them as they walked. "We think that something big is going to happen with the summit, and that's why Sayed Fahim is here in Iraq. Al-Masri can't be far behind, so when Fahim was wounded, they were desperate for medical care and were hasty in orchestrating this kidnapping. I mean, they took a lot of chances, which means they made mistakes, and that's how we'll find them." Colonel Palmer stopped in front of a small trailer. "Here's where Captain Shepherd was posted." Then he pointed to the two trailers next to it. "That is where you and Mr. Jameson will be staying, General Shepherd; your daughter will be right next door." The two military men pulled off to the side for a few moments, talking quietly between themselves. It looked like the colonel handed something to the general, but Kristen couldn't see what it was. After a moment, they saluted each other. "I'll check on you later," the colonel said as he walked away.

Kristen walked toward her trailer and opened the door, surprised to see her small suitcase already there. A cot was on one side, and she eyed it, wanting nothing more than to lie down. "Do you think they'll let us talk to that interpreter's wife?" she asked.

"Maybe," her father said, but his face didn't look hopeful. "Let's rest a bit and build up our strength; then we'll be ready for the battle." He opened the door to his trailer. "We'll see you in an hour."

Kristen nodded and went inside her trailer, kicking off her shoes and sitting on the cot. She heard a small explosion in the distance and wondered if she'd even be able to sleep. She didn't have to wonder for long. Within moments of her head hitting the soft pillow, her mind was released into slumber.

In what felt like only a few minutes, Kristen was awakened by a scratching at her door. She looked around, then cautiously got up and opened her door a crack. A girl with long black hair tied back in a bun stood outside. She motioned for Kristen to come out and pointed at the entrance to the base. Kristen shook her head, but the girl was insistent. "Come. I will help you find the doctor."

At these words, Kristen bit her lip and considered knocking on Ryan's door. The girl followed her gaze and shook her head. "No. Only you."

"You know where my brother is?" she asked, slipping on her shoes. The girl nodded. "Then we should tell the colonel so the army can go and get him."

"No." The girl shook her head violently. "They will hurt him if the army comes."

"I can't go alone. Those people are very dangerous," Kristen argued, rubbing her eyes and trying to shake the sleep from her brain.

"You will come and help him," she said simply, starting to walk away. "Madj told me I should come for you."

At the sound of Madj's name, Kristen hurried to catch up. She was torn; this was her chance to help Brandon, but she needed to let Ryan and the others know about this new development. It was too dangerous to go alone. She looked around, thinking that maybe she could alert one of the soldiers, but Madj's words echoed in her ears. There would be consequences. She groaned inwardly, not knowing exactly what to do. "How do you know where my brother is?" she asked.

The girl shrugged her shoulders. "I was told only to bring you to Madj."

"How did you get on this base?" Kristen whispered urgently. "Where is Madj?"

"I do the laundry here as a third-country national," she said. "I am from the Philippines. Everyone calls me Anna. And Madj is paying me well." She nodded to two soldiers who passed by them and continued on her way. "Come, we must hurry." Her steps quickened, and Kristen struggled to keep up. She looked back longingly at the trailer where Ryan and her father were but knew that if she didn't hurry and catch up to Anna, she would lose any chance she had of finding Brandon. And she would do anything she could to find and help her brother. She knew she was almost out of time. Passing the checkpoint, Kristen followed Anna around the corner of the base. As soon as they were outside the walls, Anna began to run.

"Wait!" Kristen cried out. Anna looked back briefly but continued to run faster. Kristen was jerked back as she was grabbed from behind and shoved roughly against the wall. A man's hand clamped around her mouth to keep her from screaming.

"Shh," he whispered, his voice thick with an accent. "I need you to be very quiet."

CHAPTER 13

Brandon Shepherd had never felt so miserable. As Sayed Fahim's life hung by a thread, Mofak and his guards forced Brandon and Rachel to their knees, their rifles pointed at the backs of their heads. Brandon had reached for Rachel's hand and squeezed his eyes shut, waiting for the fatal moment. When it hadn't come, he opened them and was surprised to see Sayed Fahim weakly reaching toward them, motioning for Mofak to stop. They were hauled to their feet and pushed back to Sayed's bedside.

For the last three nights, their ankles had been chained to the floor on opposite ends of the room, the chains only long enough to allow them to reach the bedside of their patient while kneeling. They'd almost lost him several times, and their captors had taken great joy in putting guns to their heads and threatening them with each close call. Once, one of the guards had even pulled the trigger, but Brandon and Rachel only heard a click. The guard had laughed uproariously, and Brandon felt nauseated. With Rachel chained on the other side of the room, the only place they could actually meet and touch was at the bedside of Sayed Fahim.

Every so often Brandon heard jets overhead, and he hoped the United States was still looking for them. With each passing day, his hope dwindled a little, but he tried hard not to let Rachel know it. She was struggling enough as it was. He rubbed his neck, his gaze falling on their guard. The man watched them carefully, listening to every conversation. Brandon and Rachel had tried to talk to him at first, but all he would tell them was his name—Akmal. They'd finally given up trying to engage him in conversation and mostly just pretended he wasn't there.

Brandon took out his Book of Mormon and held it between his hands. Mofak had found it on Brandon, but when Brandon had explained it was a holy book to him, Mofak had let him keep it. With nothing else to do but swelter in the oppressive heat and watch over their sleeping patient, Brandon and Rachel had taken to reading it aloud to each other to pass the time. He found great comfort within its pages, knowing the Lord hadn't forgotten him. Still, it was hard to be patient.

"Are you going to read?" Rachel asked from across the room.

He nodded. "Yeah. It was getting pretty exciting when we left off, don't you think?" he asked with a smile.

"I think Ammon had them on the run when we last stopped reading." Rachel smiled back. "Maybe if we offer to be Sayed's servants, he'll make us an offer like the Lamanite king did to Ammon. What do you think?"

"I don't know, I suppose they could make you his wife, and I'd become your sheep farmer or something," he told her. He opened the book and turned the pages. "You know, at first this book just seemed like a story to me, but the more I read, the more I realized it was more than that. Take the Ammon story, for example. He reminds me that all people have to find their spiritual way here on this earth— even the people that don't seem worth saving." He stole a glance at Sayed, and Akmal's eyes followed. "We are all worth a great deal in God's eyes."

Akmal snorted and looked over at the sleeping man, then back at Brandon, his lips twisted into a sneer. "You see him as the world sees him." He looked away, then turned back sharply, putting his gun down beside him with a clatter. He looked up at Brandon, his deep brown eyes solemn. "Despite your blindness with Sayed, we are similar, you know."

Both Rachel and Brandon turned to look at him in surprise. Brandon was first to recover. "What?"

"We are similar," Akmal repeated. "The Quran teaches that we must follow God's laws, just like your book does." He pointed to the small book in Brandon's hand. "And I see you pray often when you think I am not looking. We are similar."

"I'm surprised you speak English," Rachel said. "Why wouldn't you speak to us before?"

"Of course I speak English," Akmal answered, sounding somewhat offended. "And I had nothing to say to you before. I listen to you read this book. I know it is important to you. I feel the same about my holy book." He sat back, moving his gun closer to his side before turning away from them. "I did not think you would be like this. I did not think you were like me."

Brandon looked at Rachel and raised his eyebrows. He shrugged his shoulders in surprise. Neither of them knew what to say. Neither did Akmal, who picked up his gun and resumed his post near the door.

Rachel was the first to break the silence and continued with the conversation that Brandon had started. "I think Ammon saw how similar people were no matter what religion they subscribed to, and he just tried to serve them." She fell quiet again, glancing over at Akmal before continuing. "You know, Brandon, I understand now how you were able to follow your conscience when it came to Sayed's treatment."

At her tone of voice, Brandon motioned with his head toward Sayed and started toward the bed. She followed his example, meeting him there. They knelt across from each other, with Sayed between them. They hadn't talked about this since that first night. "I'm relieved. I know it was hard for you to understand why I couldn't let Sayed die." He looked her in the eye, glad she'd opened the discussion again. "I knew what you were thinking when we read the story of Nephi and Laban and the scripture that talked about letting one man die to save a nation. But that's so different from the situation we're facing. The Lord knew that the records Laban refused to give up were important, so He prepared a way for Nephi to save generations of people from spiritual death. But I haven't been given Nephi's duties, so I can't let Sayed die—it would be murder to me."

Rachel nodded. "I agree. I just never thought I'd have a terrorist's life in my hands. It's been overwhelming." Her voice was low and husky, and he felt she wanted to say more. After a minute's silence, she finally spoke. "Why don't you let me read this time?"

Handing the book to Rachel, his fingers brushed against hers, the touch sending tingles up his arm. She took the book, watching their hands, then slowly let her eyes travel up to his face. She watched him, saying so much while saying nothing at all. Finally, she swallowed as if the words were stuck. Biting her lip, she gave him a small smile. "Thank you, Brandon—for everything."

He looked at her and felt a rush of admiration; here she was, exhausted and as dirty as she was, kneeling over the bed of a terrorist, smiling and thanking him. She was one of the strongest women he'd ever met. He reached his hand toward her, palm up, returning her smile. The emotion in the room was palpable. Pushing back the long sleeves of her abayah, she tentatively reached out and put her hand in his. He squeezed her hand, turning it over and letting his thumb brush over the back. "Rachel, you don't have to thank me for anything."

She looked away, the color in her cheeks blazing, and Brandon grinned. He wished he wasn't chained to a floor, but it was probably a good thing. He wanted to be near her more than he had wanted anything in his entire life—to be able to run his hand along her jawline and look into her eyes as he bent slowly to kiss her. He could vividly imagine her soft lips against his. Taking a deep breath, he looked away. Covering his thoughts, he dropped her hand to check Sayed's pulse. "I think he'll be ready to travel soon."

Rachel watched him, a bemused look on her face. Brandon could tell she knew what he was trying to do, but she played along. "I think so, too. What do you think they're going to do with us?"

"I haven't let my thoughts go there," he confessed softly. "I'm afraid they aren't going to be taking us with them, if you know what I mean." Brandon still hoped that whatever happened he and Rachel would be able to face it together. He thought of his own family and wondered what Kristen and his dad would think of Rachel. Rachel's head covering was askew, and she wore no makeup of any kind. She was beautiful to him. He admired her courage and fortitude as well as her grace under pressure. She'd been amazing throughout the entire ordeal. "Well, at least we're together, and hopefully, we'll be together until the end." He knew it sounded ominous, and he hoped it didn't come to that. Rachel closed her eyes and lowered her head without saying anything.

Akmal got up from his post as another guard entered the room, balancing a tray in his arms. "Is it lunch time already?" Brandon asked. "It's so hard to tell. Days and nights are all melting together for me in this heat."

Without a word, the guard put the tray down next to Brandon on the floor, nodded at Akmal, and left. Brandon hoped in vain that it wasn't the same mush they'd been fed the entire time they'd been there. It was; however, there were two bowls instead of the customary one. "Hey, it must be two-for-one day," Brandon observed, pointing at the second bowl. "I won't have to share with you."

"I was the one sharing with you," she teased back as she stretched her ankle chain to reach over the bed and take her bowl. "If I had let you go first, there wouldn't have been any for me."

Brandon reached over and handed a bowl to Rachel before taking his own, and they both sat on the floor to eat. Since they only received one meal a day, Brandon held his breath at the rank smell of their meal and ate it hungrily. He had learned to down the mush quickly so he wouldn't actually taste much of it. Rachel did the same. The food didn't smell or look good, but it was all they had. When their bowls were empty, they settled back against the wall, using it as a backrest. "Those MREs are sounding pretty good about now, aren't they?" he said ruefully.

Rachel laughed. "I never thought I'd say that, but yes. I'd give my right arm for an MRE right now." She rubbed her stomach. "I'm so hungry I'd eat anything I got my hands on."

"Well, that's probably why they won't let *us* feed Sayed." Brandon's tone was sarcastic. Their patient received meat and vegetables, and Akmal was required to feed him. "I guess it's to build up his strength, though, so I shouldn't begrudge him."

Rachel began to flip through the pages of the Book of Mormon. "I try not to think about it," she said, moving around, obviously trying to find a comfortable position. "Let's read." She started where they'd left off, with the Anti-Nephi-Lehies being protected by the armies of Nephites. She stopped reading halfway through one verse. "Do you think the people of Iraq will ever know safety and peace like these people?" she asked softly.

"That's part of the reason we're here, isn't it?" he said, leaning over to see her more clearly from across the room. "To protect the Iraqi people and help them in their struggle for freedom."

"But there's so much suffering. Look at little Yusuf." She hurried on before emotion could overtake her. "He'll never be the same."

"None of us will ever be the same." Brandon moved back to the bed, and Rachel did as well. He reached for her hand, and she immediately held hers out to him. He smiled and gave her hand a small squeeze. Straining at the chain that had him bound, Brandon tried to give her some small comfort. "We have to believe we're making a difference here." He lightly stroked the back of her hand. "Rachel, I . . ."

Before he could finish, Sayed Fahim reached up and put his hand over both of theirs. He tried to raise himself off the bed and pointed at the book in Rachel's hand. "Don't strain yourself," Rachel told him. "Lie down." She pushed him back gently, and he obeyed.

Sayed pointed at the book again. Rachel started to hand it to him, but he held up his hand and pointed to her. "You want me to read?" she asked. When he nodded, Rachel raised her eyebrows. Brandon returned her surprised gaze.

Akmal grunted and walked over to Sayed's bedside. "He doesn't understand English, he only likes the sound of your voices." He gave them a cursory glance, then addressed Brandon directly. "Do you believe the Bible?"

Brandon nodded. "Yes."

"As well as this book you read from?"

Again, Brandon nodded.

Akmal seemed to weigh this information, running a hand over his beard. "I also believe in the Bible as well as the Quran." He looked over at Brandon, shook his head, and retraced his steps to his position at the door. "You may read to him now if that's what he wishes," he told them, laying his gun over his lap.

Brandon was surprised by Akmal's questions and not quite sure what to make of them. But if his answers made him and Rachel more human to their guards, he was all for a religious discussion.

Rachel read for half an hour more until the light was gone. Sayed seemed to fall back asleep as soon as she started reading, and Brandon imagined that her voice was soothing to him, just as Akmal thought. She closed the book, and Brandon was surprised when Akmal stood up and left, leaving them alone. Rachel looked over at the sleeping man on the bed, her forehead wrinkled, and it was apparent that she had something on her mind. "What do you think brought him to this point in his life?" she asked, looking at Sayed Fahim's face, peaceful in slumber.

"I don't know. And I'm not sure if I want to know. I just want us to get out of here safely." Brandon stopped for a moment, watching her carefully before he bent and kissed the back of her hand. She flushed, and he clasped her fingers between his own. "Rachel, these past few days have really driven home the importance of valuing each moment in my life and not being so cavalier about it. I want you to know I . . . well, I really care about . . ." He took a deep breath and rushed on. "I've really come to care for you."

Her eyes seemed to glow, reflecting the small amount of light the room boasted, and he realized there were tears glistening in them. "I care for you, too, Brandon." She put her other hand over his, and they stayed still for a moment, looking at each other.

He smiled and tried to reach over the bed to kiss her. It was awkward with the patient between them and the chains that held them not permitting them to be close enough. He wished he could hold her in his arms, and he sighed with frustration, pulling on the chain around his ankle. Whispering Rachel's name, he reached out and touched her cheek. She leaned into him, closing her eyes at the contact.

"We should probably get some sleep," he said reluctantly. She nodded, tilting her head as if she didn't want the moment to end. He pulled back. "I'll take the first watch tonight," he offered, and Rachel agreed.

They separated, and he walked barefoot back to the corner, dragging his chain behind him. He leaned back against the concrete wall, trying to arch his back and find a comfortable position with the chain around his ankle. It was frustrating to be without his boots, but he understood why Mofak had taken them after he and Rachel had tried to escape the first time. It would be hard to get very far in this part of the country without boots, and Mofak knew it.

With Sayed finally starting to show some improvement, Mofak seemed to be more relaxed, although Brandon had heard him mutter about how the Americans were closing in and how they should have been gone by then. It had made Brandon's hope soar. But as the days wore on and rescue did not seem imminent, his hope was lagging. He kept telling himself it had to be simply a matter of time, but the issue was whether they had time.

* * *

Rachel curled up as best she could on the floor, looking at the small book in her hand. Never in her wildest dreams would she have imagined herself reading it. She believed in science—things and theories she could prove and experiment with, but the words on each page had the ring of truth, and she felt comforted somehow. She needed them. Her mind was filled with "what if" scenarios. She was, after all, chained to a floor, barefoot, and wearing an abayah. The freedom she had enjoyed as an American woman had been all but taken from her. She wasn't wearing practical clothes, she was no longer allowed to speak in Mofak's presence unless she had permission, and she was a prisoner.

The chance of a rescue looked more and more bleak with each passing day, and she wondered whether they would ever be found. Rachel thought of her grandmother and was glad that she wasn't alive to worry about her. No one would worry since she had no living relatives. No one had worried about her for a long time—until Brandon. She glanced over at him. Their connection had grown stronger over the last few days, and her feelings of gratitude had started to turn into something more. She tried not to let the fact that the chances of ever being able to act on or explore those feelings seemed slim and concentrated instead on the fact that she had him here now, and that they were alive and together. Closing her eyes, she knew he would watch over her while she slept. And then it would be her turn to watch over him. Amidst the chaos of the situation, she felt safe under Brandon's eye. She didn't let herself think beyond that but rather lived moment to moment. That was all there was. She closed her eyes and hoped sleep would come quickly.

Mere seconds seemed to have passed when Brandon's voice came to her through her dreams, urgently calling her name. "Rachel! Someone's coming!"

The room was dark, lit only by a candle, and she sat up straight, her senses immediately on alert. She could hear murmuring outside, then the door handle jiggled, and the door creaked open slightly. "Dr. Fielding?" the dark shadow called; the voice was familiar.

"Nazir? Is that you?" Rachel asked, coming toward him, dragging her chain with her.

"Yes." He came inside and shut the door. Glancing at Brandon, he made his way to Rachel. "I am sorry about this. I had no choice." He looked over at the bed and lowered his voice. "They have my sons and would have killed them if I hadn't helped them find a doctor quickly."

Rachel nodded at her chains. "Show me you are truly sorry and help us escape."

"I don't know how," he said, shaking his head sadly. "They are leaving in the morning, and I do not think they are planning to take you along."

Rachel leaned forward, trying to shake off her abayah enough so that her hands could get through the material. She touched Nazir lightly on the shoulder, trying to look him in the eye to make sure he understood her. "Can you get the key to the chains? Lead us out of this building?"

Brandon had come toward them and was straining to hear the conversation from across the room. "How many guards are here, Nazir? Are the Americans close?"

Nazir nodded his head and came closer to Brandon so he could talk softly and still be heard. "The Americans are close. They have raided the town next to us looking for you. Mofak thinks these buildings will be next, and that is why they are leaving." He glanced at the door. "There are many guards. I do not know how, but I will try to get the key." He stood. "I am an honorable man, Dr. Fielding. I would never have done anything like this except in the most desperate circumstances."

"I understand, Nazir," Rachel said. "But I'm not ready to die."

Nazir moved toward the door and opened it, bowing slightly toward Brandon and Rachel before closing it behind him.

"Do you really think he'll help us?" Brandon asked, his words floating to her in the darkness.

"I hope so," she answered back.

CHAPTER 14

Kristen was quickly hustled toward the side of the base. The man leading her kept them near the wall, so as not to arouse any suspicion, she assumed.

"Hey!"

Kristen heard a voice behind her, and realizing it was her father's, she froze. The man beside her slowly turned around, drawing a gun and pointing it at Kristen's temple.

Her father stood with his hands raised. "Don't shoot. I'm unarmed. Don't hurt her."

"I will kill her right here, right now." The man's voice was calm and clear, but Kristen could see his hand trembling. She watched her father move toward them, his steps even and calculated. "Stop right there," the man demanded, pulling her backward against him.

"Dad," she croaked out, trying to keep her voice steady. "They know where Brandon is." The barrel of the gun pressed harder against her forehead. "I just want to help my brother," she told her captor. "Please don't hurt us."

At that moment a truck came around the corner with Anna in the driver's seat. It zigzagged toward them as if the driver wasn't very experienced.

The man looked like he was debating Kristen's request. "This might be better than I thought. Get in," he ordered Kristen's father, waving the gun toward the vehicle that had stopped beside them. Kristen's father obeyed. Kristen was pushed inside and shoved to the bottom of the cab. The man with the gun got in after them, and the truck lurched forward. Kristen bit her tongue as she fell, tasting blood.

"Who are you?" she asked, trying to turn so she could see the man in the passenger seat. She was able to catch her father's eye, and he gave her an imperceptible shake of his head, telling her to be quiet. In this instance, she obeyed.

The truck bounced along for what seemed like hours. Kristen noticed that Anna's feet barely touched the pedals and that she had to stomp on the brakes to get the truck to stop, practically sliding down the seat. When the vehicle stopped, the man got out and grabbed Kristen's arm, jamming the gun in her side. "Get out," he directed the general. "You will walk in front of me. And if you try anything, you'll never see your son or your daughter again."

Kristen was practically propelled toward a small house, followed closely by her father. She looked around at the well-kept neighborhood. They were surrounded by small homes with shutters over the windows and tiny fenced yards. Kristen couldn't put her finger on it, but something wasn't quite right. She took one last glance before being forced through the door. Then it hit her. There were no sounds. No children's voices, nothing. It was like something had come along and stolen the life out of the entire neighborhood. Blinking and quickly trying to adjust to the darkness as she went over the threshold, Kristen stumbled inside. Both Kristen and her father were led to chairs in a small room and told to sit down. They did, and their hands were promptly tied behind their backs.

The man stood in the doorway with his arms folded, tapping his gun on his forearm and watching them, his eyes hooded and unreadable. Kristen put on her best game face, trying not to look as terrified as she was.

A small woman came in with two guards but she kept her face turned away from Kristen and her father. Kristen couldn't see much of her beneath the abayah she wore. She spoke to the man that had brought them in the truck. Kristen tried to eavesdrop on their conversation, hearing bits of Arabic, but all she could make out was "We got a general," and "What will Mofak say?" Then the woman left the room for a moment, the guards trailing her every step. When she returned, she smiled as she walked toward Kristen, ignoring the general. "Where is Michael?" she asked, obviously expecting an immediate answer.

"Are you Madj?" Kristen asked, knowing the answer before she asked the question. The face before her was unmistakably the one from Michael's picture. And even though that gave her a small amount of comfort, she was still frightened by their circumstances and amazed that her voice wasn't shaking with fear.

The woman stood directly in front of Kristen, the material from her head-covering falling over one shoulder, her deep brown eyes flashing. "Tell me where Michael is. Now."

Kristen raised her chin. "Tell me where my brother is."

Kristen's father started forward. "You know where my son is?"

The woman raised an eyebrow and went over to the general. "You are Captain Brandon Shepherd's father—General Grant Shepherd, yes?"

The general sat back in his seat but didn't reply.

She kicked his chair. "Answer me!"

"Yes, I am General Grant Shepherd. Where is my son?" He glared at her, willing her to answer him, but even his most commanding voice didn't seem to faze her.

Circling both of their chairs, Madj turned thoughtfully. "You worked at the Pentagon. You had the ear of the president on many defense matters," she mused as she walked. She had obviously done her research. "And you will be our ticket inside," she declared.

Madj turned and walked quickly out of the room, Kristen and her father powerless to do anything but watch her go. Looking over at her dad, Kristen gave him a questioning look, but he shrugged his shoulders. Within moments, Madj returned, a satellite phone in her hand.

She handed it to the general. "I want you to call your contacts at the Pentagon and request entry to the Security Summit that is taking place in Baghdad tomorrow. You will be the perfect person to get us in."

The general shook his head. "No. I'm not going to help you."

"Madj, please," Kristen said, straining against the ropes that bound her hands. "Just tell us where Brandon is. Don't do this."

Madj turned and slapped Kristen's cheek, her hand quicker than a snake's tongue. "Shut up. You don't know what is at stake here. You know nothing, and you have no loyalty. Michael trusted you."

"He betrayed my trust," Kristen said, pressing her stinging jaw against her shoulder, her cheek on fire.

"It was your betrayal that cost him!" Madj shouted. "Who is sitting in a prison somewhere? Not you." She sneered. "Not yet, anyway." Turning back to Kristen's father, Madj shoved the phone toward his face. "You will make the call."

The general shook his head. Madj tipped her head toward the guard, and the general braced himself for an attack. But the guards didn't come near him. Kristen was hauled to her feet, then forced to her knees directly in front of her father, who stood. Even with his hands tied behind him, Kristen thought he looked formidable. A gun was pressed against the back of her head, and she bent forward with the pressure.

"You will have her pretty little head splatted all over you in just a few moments," Madj said, her voice low. "Do as I say, and your daughter will live."

Kristen looked at her father, wondering what he would do. His usually calm exterior seemed shaken by Madj's words. He looked at Kristen with an anguished expression.

Then he closed his eyes for a moment. Snapping them back open, the look on his face told Kristen he'd made his decision. "All right, give me the phone," he said, slumping back down in his seat, not meeting Kristen's eyes.

"Your call will be monitored and traced, so don't do anything stupid," Madj told him. She circled the chair like a vulture, finally stopping to untie the general's hands. The smile on her face made Kristen's heart pound with anger as she was shoved back into her chair. "Don't do it, Dad. Don't let them win!"

He glanced at her, the phone already to his ear. "I won't let anything happen to you," he said quietly. "That's one thing you can always count on."

His words brought tears to Kristen's eyes. It was the closest he'd ever come to telling her he loved her. "Dad," she murmured softly, wanting to say so much more. He shook his head at her, hiding his own emotions by turning toward the phone.

"Get on with it," Madj demanded, breaking the moment. The general bent to his task.

They all listened to him as he attempted to set up his attendance and entry into the Summit. After almost an hour of calling in favors and using several contacts, he hung up. "It's done," he told them. "I can pick up my security pass when we reach the location."

Madj smiled. "Excellent." She took the phone from him. "We will be leaving within the hour." She left the room, and they could hear her talking excitedly on the phone to someone named Mofak. From what Kristen could make out, Mofak was Madj's older brother, and he was proud of her new plan to get into the Summit.

Kristen sighed with frustration and looked over at her father. He looked tired. "Dad," she said softly, tears gathering in her eyes again.

"It's okay, pumpkin," he said, but didn't meet her eyes. "We're going to get through this. And we're going to get through it together."

They sat in the hard chairs and looked at one another, neither speaking. Kristen didn't know what to say. He'd sacrificed his honor, the one thing she knew mattered most to him. And he'd done it for her because, in his own way, he loved her.

Madj came back into the room, her face hardly able to contain her smile. "We are set. No one ever dreamed we would have an American general to get us on the inside. It is truly providential. For us, I mean," she said as she grinned. Coming over to stand beside Kristen, her grin disappeared. She looked at Kristen from several angles, as if she were contemplating a purchase and wanted to examine the merchandise. Kristen resisted the urge to squirm. What was going on?

"We are very different," she said finally, pushing her head covering behind her ears.

Kristen nodded. "I would say so."

"But Michael loved both of us." Her voice was matter-of-fact.

"I guess so," Kristen replied, her tone just as neutral. "We've done everything you wanted. Can you tell us where my brother is, please?"

Madj blew out a breath and pulled Kristen's chin upward, forcing her to look into Madj's face. Kristen wrenched away, but Madj just shook her head. "I wanted to hurt you because Michael loved you more than me."

"You and your brother were blackmailing him," Kristen said sharply. "That's not love."

"You know nothing of what happened between us, how good we were together," Madj snapped back at her. "Michael is our family, but it is complicated." She squatted in front of Kristen, and the women's eyes locked. "Seeing you, though, makes me understand why Michael loved you."

"What do you mean?"

"There is a light in your eyes," was all Madj said. "He sees in you what he saw once in himself—idealism."

"I'm just here for my brother. Michael and I aren't together anymore, okay? I know you can help me. If you loved Michael at all, you'll help me. He gave me your name. Why would he do that if he didn't want you to help me?" She was anxious to talk, to get everything out in the open so that maybe the pieces of the puzzle would start coming together. Her stomach was in knots, but she knew she had to keep talking, not only for herself, but for Brandon. If she was going to help Brandon at all, now was the time, this was the chance. It felt like the most important interview of her entire life. She hadn't even felt this nervous when she'd gone on CNN. Closing her eyes, she tried to gather her thoughts, conjuring up a smiling image of Brandon. She needed to do this for her brother. His life depended on it.

"I can help you, but I want you to help me first," Madj said simply.

"We gave you a free pass into the Security Summit," Kristen said, raising her voice as her frustration mounted. "What more do you want?"

"I need to know where they've taken Michael so I can get him out. Just like you want to know where your brother is."

Kristen leaned forward. "The truth is, I don't know where they've taken Michael. They wouldn't tell me. The only thing I know is that he's still being questioned." Madj looked down at Kristen, searching her eyes to determine whether or not she was telling the truth. Kristen hurried on. "I love my brother more than anything. Please, if you can help me find him . . ." She stopped, trying to swallow the tears that threatened to fall.

"He is in an abandoned village thirty miles north of here. But it won't do you any good to know that. We will be in Baghdad shortly, and when Mofak no longer has a use for your brother, he will kill him."

Kristen sucked in a breath and shook her head, the thought too horrible to imagine. "We helped you—why won't you help us?"

"I *am* helping you. I'm helping you become part of the solution instead of part of the problem." Madj shook her head. "If we are successful in our mission, the United States will someday thank us for our vision and fortitude."

Kristen's father snorted at this turn in the conversation. "Do you really believe that?"

Madj nodded. "I know it is true. This solution will change your world and your worldview." She stood and motioned to the man who was just outside the door. "People will be safe again. That's all they want. Take Haidar, here. He was going about his business, repairing shoes and taking care of his family, when his nephews were kidnapped, and his brother, Nazir, disappeared. Now his life will never be the same again. He has done things he never dreamed he would do, all in the name of family and safety. If we succeed, people like Haidar won't have to suffer anymore. Everyone will enjoy the same blessings of security."

"It won't be true security. And their freedom will be taken away again," Kristen countered.

Madj shot back, "Strong leadership is what's needed. Guidance and direction."

"The people will only have effective leadership under an elected government," the general said. "That's what we're all fighting to achieve. Freedom to choose who leads you and where."

"The price is too high, and the sooner people realize that, the better. The masses are like sheep—they need the shepherd to tell them how to have a good life." Madj was pacing now, her voice raised. "They wander aimlessly because they don't know what to do with freedom, and it ruins the focus for the country. One person can bring it all together, concentrate the strength, and raise us up as an example to the world."

"You won't succeed. Freedom will win," Kristen said confidently.

"That's where you're wrong." Madj stopped pacing. "And you will be part of our success by helping us to raid that Summit." She turned on her heel. "Get them in the trucks," she instructed Haidar.

Madj disappeared into the hall, and Haidar jerked Kristen and her father to their feet. He moved them toward the back of the house, opposite the way they'd come in. Kristen tried to catch her father's eye to see if he was planning on trying to make a run for it, but he was staring at Haidar. "Don't do this," she heard her father say.

Haidar didn't respond, just shoved him toward the door. As they went outside, Kristen squinted in the brightness after being in the darkened house. When she heard a loud popping noise in front of her, she instinctively ducked. Haidar was shooting at someone! He grabbed her father and began using him as a shield against possible return fire. "Don't shoot!" Kristen shouted, wishing she could see who Haidar was shooting at and hoping they didn't shoot back and hit her father.

"Stay back, Kristen!" her father shouted, twisting his neck to see her. Haidar waved his gun as he started moving toward the truck a few feet away. He kept the general squarely in front of him. Kristen didn't know what to do. Should she follow them?

"Run!" her father shouted. "Get out of here now!"

Kristen looked over at the house across the street and saw a man wearing the uniform of a U.S. Marine moving toward her. His eyes locked with hers, then flicked to Haidar. If she ran, would Haidar shoot her? She was rooted to the spot where she stood, unable to decide on a course of action. Suddenly, the soldier in front of her raised his weapon. She stood open-mouthed as he squeezed the trigger.

Closing her eyes, she waited for the bullet to hit, but then she heard it whiz by her. Turning around, she saw Madj fall to the ground, holding her shoulder.

"Shoot them!" Madj yelled to Haidar. "Shoot them all!" But before Haidar could react, they were surrounded by soldiers in full-body armor. Kristen felt the adrenaline surge through her, and she pushed through toward her father. "Dad!" she shouted.

"I'm here," he said as they watched Haidar being taken into custody.

"Come with me," the soldier closest to them commanded. Kristen and her father obeyed, and as they came around the corner of the house, they both gaped in amazement. Military vehicles were everywhere; Kristen marveled at the fact that they hadn't heard a thing inside the house. The silence from before was gone as people milled about, securing each house along the road. Looking back,

Kristen caught a glimpse of Haidar, now splayed on the ground, and Madj, who appeared to be getting medical attention for her wound. Anna was sitting beside the house as they came out front, her arms around her knees.

The general squatted down in front of Anna. "How do you know these people?" he asked her as he rubbed his wrists from the rope burn.

She didn't look up but spoke quietly. "He is Haidar Moussa. He is my father's best friend."

The general tightened his lips and stood, helping Anna to her feet. "Come with me," he told the girl. Colonel Palmer was waiting by the truck, watching the exchange. He knit his eyebrows together but didn't say anything to the general. When they were all seated, they started back for the base. Kristen was silent as they drove, the adrenaline still pumping through her. Finally, she asked, "Why did you follow me, Dad?"

"Someone had to have the sense to follow you," he growled. "It was a good thing I did." He sighed and turned slightly to face her. "Agent Lewis told me about Michael mentioning Madj. We knew a little about her, but Agent Lewis warned me to watch for a possible contact between the two of you. When I heard your door open, I figured it was her."

Kristen turned her head away. "So you've known all along?"

"I knew some things. I wish you had trusted me with the rest." He watched the bland scenery going by and turned his face away. "I didn't want to see you hurt, so I tried to protect you. Just like I assume you thought you were protecting Brandon by not telling me about this woman." He slowly let out a breath. "I clued the colonel in as soon as I could and told him about the possibility of you being contacted, but frankly, we were surprised that someone on base was able to get to you so easily. I had a tracking device on, so I wasn't worried when I followed you and we were taken. I knew we'd be found eventually, but I needed to make sure we were going to get out of this alive. It wouldn't have helped anyone to lead the army to our bodies."

"But what about the phone calls you made?" she asked.

"That was all real, actually. I didn't know how sophisticated their equipment was, and I couldn't risk your life. I am cleared to attend the Summit." He patted her arm. "I'm sure we'll have Brandon back by then and be on our way home." He leaned forward and addressed Colonel Palmer. "We're going to have to alert Washington that this group plans to raid the Summit." The colonel nodded. "Oh, and we have Brandon's location."

At that, the colonel turned around, his eyes wide.

"Let's go get him," was all he said.

They made it back to base and headed straight for the hospital. Several soldiers came to help, taking the girl from the Humvee and waiting to treat the prisoners. When Kristen and her father got into the triage area, Kristen saw Ryan coming toward them. A shadow of concern crossed his face when he saw the condition they were in and the crowd of excited soldiers.

"What happened?" Ryan asked when he was finally able to reach them. "I've been looking everywhere for you two. No one seemed to know anything."

The general sat down heavily on a chair. He mopped his brow, sighing in the heat. "Kristen was taken off base for a meeting with the group that has Brandon. I followed her." He glanced over at her, and for the first time in what seemed like forever, Kristen felt like she and her father were on the verge of coming to an understanding with each other. "I couldn't let both my children be taken, never to see them again," he murmured, his voice barely audible over the hospital's sounds. He wiped his brow on his sleeve, and it dawned on Kristen that Brandon had a habit of doing the same thing. "It's hotter than Hades in here," he commented.

"Can I get you something to drink, General?" one soldier offered. The general nodded, and the soldier quickly left.

Ryan tightened his lips as he moved toward Kristen. "How did this happen?"

"Madj had a girl contact me." From the look on Ryan's face, she could tell exactly what he was thinking. "I wanted to go and get you, but there was no time."

His brow furrowed, the shock registering in his eyes. "You took a big risk. Couldn't you have yelled, alerted someone, anything?" His fists clenched as he spoke.

Kristen thought of the soldiers she had passed and how close she'd been to Ryan's trailer. "I'm sorry. I was afraid I'd spook her and we'd lose our only chance to find Brandon," Kristen said, closing her eyes against the guilty feeling that washed over her. "It turned out okay."

Ryan's expression was incredulous, but he didn't say another word. He turned on his heel, wrenching open the door and slamming it shut as he left.

Kristen's father patted her knee. "He's only upset because he cares for you, pumpkin."

Kristen's mouth hung open. She hadn't heard her father call her "pumpkin" in years, and this was the second time today. "Dad . . ." she began, but they were suddenly surrounded by medics, circling around Madj as a Humvee arrived and she was escorted into a back room. Kristen shuddered at the look Madj gave her as she passed by.

The general watched the medics go, then turned to look at Kristen. "Let's go see what the plan is to get Brandon." He took her by the arm, led her down the hall to the colonel's office, and knocked. Then he entered without waiting for an invitation. The colonel was inside and held up his hand as he finished a phone call.

"What will happen to Madj?" Kristen asked as soon as he set the phone down, her curiosity getting the better of her.

"She will be questioned and held," Colonel Palmer replied without preamble. "Hopefully she will lead us to others in her organization. Now, show me," he indicated a map, "where we can find Brandon and Rachel." Both Kristen and the general looked at the map for several minutes, finally pinpointing one area. "She said there's an abandoned village here. That's where they are."

The colonel sprang into action, picking up his phone again and giving as many details as he could. "Thanks. I'll let you know what we find out," he said to the general during a pause in his phone conversation.

Kristen and her father went back to the hospital's waiting room, unsure what to do with themselves. The place seemed to be a hotbed of activity at the moment. Kristen watched several patients come in for treatment—some for horrific injuries. She could hardly believe what was happening around her. Helicopter rotors reverberated outside, and the telltale clanging of a bell signaled the hospital staff to move outside and pick up new patients. There was a steady stream of two-wheeled, metal, rickshaw-like litters brought into the area next to where Kristen and her father waited. Several injured soldiers walked to a corner area while the more critical patients were taken to separate rooms. Kristen saw one wounded soldier grabbing a medic and asking for information. "How's my buddy?" he said softly.

"I'll try and find out for you," the medic said before moving away to tend to more wounded.

Kristen's heart ached for the soldiers around her. She understood Brandon's need to try to help, because she felt like she should be doing more herself. "Do you think Brandon sees this every day?" she asked her father as she sat down.

"Probably," he told her. "That's part of war."

"It's an ugly part," she said. "I'm glad Brandon can at least make it better for some." She paused. "Do you think he's still alive?"

Her father turned to look at her. "Yes, I do. And you have to believe that too." His voice was forceful, the tone she remembered growing up, and she immediately felt defensive.

Kristen took a breath and bit her tongue. Her first reaction was a desire to tell her father that he couldn't *order* her to feel a certain way. But a larger part of her realized that her emotions were too close to the surface, and she didn't want to break the fragile line of communication she and her father finally seemed to be sharing.

"Don't you think the sacrifice is too great?" she finally murmured, thinking out loud as she watched some of the litter bearers bend to scoop up soiled desert camouflage uniforms and mop the blood off of the floor.

He patted her arm. "Sometimes," he said softly. She could tell his thoughts were of his son, a prisoner of war. She wanted to say something to comfort him, but she couldn't think of anything. No matter how badly she wanted a connection, the truth was that so many years of distance between them had taken their toll.

"I think I'll go find Ryan," she said, standing and making her way to the door. The hospital suddenly seemed oppressive, and she needed to be outside. Her father nodded and leaned back in his chair, closing his eyes. Kristen watched him for a moment, then walked out the door.

Walking toward the large tents, she made another turn and barely missed running into Ryan as he came around the corner. He held a cup in his hand. "I brought you some water," he said. "I thought it might help. And it's sort of a peace offering."

He gave it to her, and she took it gratefully. Sipping it, she grimaced. "Doesn't taste like the water back home, does it?"

Ryan smiled. "No, it doesn't." He put his hands in his pockets and bent his head. "I'm sorry I walked out on you earlier. I . . ." He raised his head and looked her straight in the eye, his eyes searching hers. "I haven't ever felt panic like that—I mean, when I realized how close you might have come to being killed. These people mean business, and you went to meet them alone. If it hadn't been for your father . . ." He shuddered involuntarily. "I don't know what I'd do if I lost you. I need you in my life, Kristy." He paused. "If you want me." Reaching out to touch her hair, he heaved a long sigh and pulled her close.

Kristen's heart was racing. She felt happy and jittery all at the same time. Had Ryan Jameson just said he needed her? It couldn't be! But he had. She smiled and held him tighter, feeling secure in his embrace. "You won't lose me, Ryan. You never have to worry about that." She tucked her head under his chin and pressed herself deeper into his embrace. Any last vestiges of doubt melted away in that moment.

He stroked her hair, tipped her face upward, then caressed her cheek, watching her carefully. She looked into his deep green eyes and never wanted the moment to end. His head lowered, and his lips brushed hers lightly. Then the kiss deepened and became more insistent. She matched his fervor, wanting him to feel what she felt for him. When they broke apart, they were both breathless. He touched his forehead to hers.

They were quiet for a few moments, but then Kristen realized that he didn't know yet about Brandon. "Did you hear? They know where Brandon is, and they're mounting a covert operation to rescue him," she said.

Ryan stood very still, then hugged her tightly. "That's great news."

"I hope we're not too late," Kristen said.

He pulled back slightly and let his finger trail over her jawline as he watched her with an intensity she'd never seen before. "We won't be. Trust me."

She smiled and held his palm against her cheek.

Their moment of quiet was shattered when several Humvees fired up, and the entire area came alive with the activity—men talked excitedly, knowing they were going after a fellow soldier. Kristen and Ryan walked back to the hospital area, Ryan holding her hand as if he didn't want to break their contact just yet.

"They're going after him now," the general said when they drew closer. "They should be there in less than an hour."

"What can we do?" Ryan asked, his face filled with concern.

"Sit and wait and pray for good news," the general replied, running a hand over the stubble on his cheeks.

Ryan turned back to Kristen. "Do you want to go back to your trailer and try to rest?" he asked softly. "No one would think less of you if you did. You've been through a lot in the past few hours."

"There's no way. I can't rest now." She watched the teams moving out, unable to keep her eyes off the men and women who might be able to save her brother's life. Ryan stood beside her, their shoulders almost touching as they listened to helicopter blades starting up. She squeezed Ryan's hand tightly. "This is it," she said, looking at Ryan. He nodded and drew her close to him as they both watched Brandon's would-be rescuers fade into the horizon.

CHAPTER 15

Brandon lay on the concrete floor, knowing that when daylight came, he and Rachel would most likely be killed unless Nazir helped them. He rubbed his hand over his growing hair, the sweat of the day evaporating in the cool of the night. It was strange how calm he felt in the face of it all. He thought of home, his parents, his childhood with Kristen, and his friendship with Ryan Jameson. He thought of how much he wanted to share his newfound faith with his family and hoped he would have the chance. He thought about how of all the things he'd accomplished and done in his life, when it came right down to it, the most important things were the relationships that he'd formed. Opening his eyes, he turned his head toward Rachel. She had quickly become very important to him.

He heard footsteps coming down the hall, and he sat up as Nazir entered the room. The interpreter went directly to Rachel, and Brandon crawled toward them so he could hear better. The chain made a scraping noise on the floor behind him, and he lifted it so the guard who was now sitting outside the door wouldn't wonder what they were doing. "You must hurry. We don't have a lot of time. I have the key." Nazir fished a small key out of his pocket and squatted down, handing it to Rachel. "If you have a chance to escape, take it. The Americans are close by, so head west." He stood. "I've done all I can."

"What did you tell the guards? What do they think you're doing in here?" Rachel asked as she fiddled with the chain around her ankle.

"There's only one guard out there now, since Mofak has all the men getting ready to move out. There's a booby trap on the front door, so don't go that way. Try to make it to the back door on the lower level," he advised. "I'm supposed to be getting Sayed ready to travel. Is there anything I should know?" He glanced over to the bed for the first time.

"No, just move him slowly so the stitches don't rip," Rachel said. "He should be fine." She touched Nazir's shoulder. "Thank you for taking this risk for us." She went back to fumbling with her chain and finally succeeded in getting it off. "Tell me, have your boys been set free?"

He nodded, his eyes darting between her and the door. "I must go. Mofak is keeping a close eye on everyone."

"Okay, then. Good luck, Nazir," Rachel said. He quickly left, softly shutting the door behind him. Akmal was outside, but he barely glanced at them.

Rachel unwrapped the chain from around her, setting it carefully to the side. She brought the key to Brandon. "Here," she said, her voice low as she kept an eye on the door. "How do you think we should get out of here?"

"There are two of us, so the odds are good that we might be able to overpower one guard," Brandon said as he worked on getting the chain from around his ankle. "I don't think the window is an option, since we're on the second floor."

Rachel went over to the window and looked out. It was a sheer drop to the courtyard below. "You're right. We're going to have to take our chances with Akmal." Rachel paused and looked back at Brandon. "I can see the sun starting to peek over the horizon. We'd better get a move on."

Finally free, Brandon stood up, flexing his ankle as he did so. He wished he had his boots back. He dreaded the thought of walking on the hot sand in bare feet—if they made it that far.

He strode to the window where Rachel stood. The sun sent its bright rays into the room, cutting through the darkness of the night. Her face was lit, and for a moment, her brown eyes were luminous, larger than usual; they seemed to look right into his soul. He stood before her, watching her for a moment before finally gathering her into his arms. "I've wanted to do this for a long time," he whispered into her hair. "No matter what happens today, Rachel, I want you to know how much I've come to care for you. If nothing else, this experience has taught me to seize the moment." And with that, he bent and kissed her tenderly, holding her in his arms and hoping he would never have to let her go. He felt her tremble and knew she was experiencing the same depth of emotion that he did. His heart soared. Breaking away, he touched her lips lightly one more time before stepping back.

"I must look a sight," she said, running a hand over her face. "It's been so hot and . . ."

"You're beautiful," he murmured, cutting her off. He wanted to kiss her again but reluctantly decided against it. "We better get out of here."

A flash of light from the courtyard momentarily blinded them, illuminating the room they'd spent the last few days chained in. Suddenly there was shouting, and smoke began to pour in from everywhere. Brandon pulled Rachel to the floor. "Looks like the cavalry's here," he said, "and they must have found the booby trap." He stood up and moved toward the door, cracking it open and motioning for Rachel to get back. Opening the door wider, he came face-to-face with Akmal, who stood in front of them, his gun pointed at Brandon's chest. Brandon slowly raised his hands. The two men stared at each other, neither one moving. Brandon saw something flicker in Akmal's eyes, and the guard's words, *we are similar,* echoed in Brandon's mind. Akmal's walkie-talkie crackled and broke the silence between them. He didn't answer the call, snapping it off quickly. Finally, he jerked his gun toward the hall. "Go!" he said sharply.

Brandon didn't question him, and he and Rachel moved quickly down the hall. They hadn't gone far when they made it to a small stairway and heard someone coming up. Brandon flattened himself against the wall, waiting for just the right moment before he punched the approaching guard. Caught by surprise, the man flew backward. Hitting his head on the concrete floor, he was knocked unconscious.

Brandon shook his hand. "Ouch!" he exclaimed, rubbing his knuckles. "That hurt a lot more than I thought it would."

"Better not damage those hands if you can help it," Rachel warned. She picked up the rifle. "You're a surgeon, after all. Let's go."

After going down the stairway the guard had come up, they found themselves in another long hallway. They could hear more explosions and then footsteps. "Which way?" Brandon whispered, looking at the maze of rooms before them. "We need to find the stairway to the lower level."

Rachel held a finger to her lips. They could clearly hear Mofak speaking from a room two doors down. "Kill the American doctors and load Sayed now," he said, his voice authoritative. "We must not be captured. It will take the soldiers some time to find this wing of the house, but we must hurry."

Rachel pointed to the door of an empty room beside them, and Brandon nodded. They slipped inside, tiptoeing in their bare feet. Holding the door slightly closed, they waited until the guards had cleared the hall. Through the crack in the door, they watched Mofak come out and look around. Then he walked quickly toward the stairway up to the room where Sayed was recuperating.

* * *

When it looked like the coast was clear, Rachel led the way out. Turning toward the room where Mofak had been, she quickly ran down the long passageway and found the stairway to the main wing of the house. Brandon was close behind. "Do you know where you're going?" Brandon whispered. She held up her hand. The explosions sounded like they were coming from the north side of the house and were getting closer.

"I think we should follow the explosions," she explained, cocking the gun. She looked at his confused expression. "That will be our best bet."

"Toward the explosions?" Brandon asked incredulously.

"We don't want to give away our position," she admonished, shushing him. She flipped around at the sound of footsteps coming up another stairway and pointed the gun. Brandon faded back against the wall. A man in camouflage was coming up the stairs; Rachel recognized him as the guard from the truck—the man that had attacked her. Anger welled within her. She thought of other women he might have hurt. She glanced briefly at Brandon, who gave her a questioning look. He couldn't see who was coming up the stairs.

Rachel sucked her breath in through her teeth. She had to make a decision. As he came closer, she raised the barrel, sighting him in. Her finger was on the trigger. All she had to do was pull. Her finger twitched, and she watched him turn away, not even noticing them. Hesitating only a moment, she lowered the gun and took a deep, gulping breath, as if she'd just come up for air.

Brandon put his hand on her arm as he watched the man enter a room. "You did the right thing, Rachel."

She closed her eyes and sagged against him. "I almost killed him." He held her and stroked her hair for a moment before she straightened. "I wanted to. I really did. But . . . well, I'm trusting you that he'll answer for his actions. Just like Sayed. Just like me," she whispered. "I can't explain why I believe you, but I do."

Brandon rubbed her arms. "I know. Let's get out of here, though, and then we'll talk about it. Over dinner, perhaps?" He grinned, and she smiled back, hoping they'd really get to fulfill that wish. She offered the gun to Brandon as he started down the stairs, carefully checking whether their field of vision was clear.

"If we follow the explosions, we'll find the rescue team," she said as she carefully followed behind him.

They made it to the lower level and looked out at a scene of mass pandemonium. They ducked into a room, closed the door until they could just see out the crack, and assessed the situation as best they could from their vantage point. Men were running and shouting; they seemed to be flowing from a doorway at the end of the hall.

"How are we going to get out of this?" Brandon asked, letting out a breath. "If they see us, they'll kill us."

"We just have to stay alive long enough for the rescue team to find us," Rachel said.

Smoke was starting to come under the door they were standing by, and Brandon opened it a little wider. "Now's our chance," he said. Rachel stayed close as they moved forward. He paused at every doorway, carefully checking before inching forward. They reached the corner and were about to move around it when shots rang out, causing concrete to splinter off the wall next to them. Both Rachel and Brandon jumped back, taking cover behind the corner. "Stay right behind me, Rachel!" Brandon said as he returned fire. He pulled the trigger several times, the deafening roar reverberating around them.

"Okay." he said. "When I shoot this time, you run for the other side of the hall. I'll be right behind you."

"No way. We stay together. Take the shot, then we'll both make a run for it."

He nodded and waited for any return fire from around the corner. He didn't have to wait long. Small concrete shards popped all around their feet as their attacker shot several rounds.

"Okay, go!" he said, and Rachel began to run. She stumbled several times as she stepped on the small concrete fragments, daggers to her bare feet. But they couldn't slow down. Rachel knew that if they did, they were dead.

They made it to the end of the hall and yanked open the door. Rachel looked back and saw a small trail of bloody footprints and knew that Brandon's feet were as lacerated as hers. Rachel turned and then stopped abruptly. When Brandon came through the door, he nearly bowled her over. He froze when he saw that her hands were raised in the face of the gun now pointing at them through the smoke.

CHAPTER 16

Ryan had gone to get everyone something to eat, and Kristen sat down next to her father. "How are you holding up?" she asked, wanting to reach out to him in some way but not daring to just yet.

He turned to look at her, and for the first time, she noticed how much older he looked; his wrinkles and gray hair were much more pronounced than she remembered. When had that happened? "I'm fine," he said. "What about you? Are you okay?"

She nodded, wanting to reassure him and take the worry from of his eyes. "I'm tired. I want this whole thing to be over." She shifted in her chair and put her hand on his arm. "We've been through a lot in the last few days. It's been eye-opening."

He glanced at her, then looked down at her hand on his arm. "Yes, it has."

Kristen looked down and pulled back, twisting her hands in her lap. "Dad, I really want us to try to get along. I know our relationship hasn't been an easy one, but with this whole situation, I've realized I haven't really been fair to you."

Her father watched her for a moment, then gently took one of her hands in his. "You remind me so much of your mother."

"What happened to us, Dad?" Kristen asked, looking earnestly into her father's eyes. "How did we grow so far apart?"

He dropped his gaze and turned away at her question, and Kristen removed her hand, hurt at his reaction. She thought about walking away but knew that this was likely the closest they would come to clearing the air. "Dad?"

He was silent for a moment, then began to speak without looking at her. "I probably wasn't cut out to be a father. The military was all I knew. But your mother brought out something softer in me, and she was so happy being with you and Brandon. When she died, it felt like all my happiness died with her, and I withdrew back into what I knew—the army. But it didn't make for being a very good father." He leaned forward and rested his elbows on his knees. Looking back at Kristen, he shook his head and said, "I'm sorry. I truly am sorry."

She leaned forward to match his stance and looked in his face. "I'm sorry too. I've just always felt that I could never be what you truly wanted. That you could never be proud of me."

He took a deep breath. "Nothing is further from the truth. I mean, you make decisions that I don't agree with, and sometimes I don't express my feelings very well, but I'm always proud of you."

Taking his words at face value, Kristen nodded. All of her life she'd wanted to have this conversation with her father, but now that it was here, it was a little disconcerting.

He continued without noticing her hesitation. "I threw myself into my job at the Pentagon; I wasn't there for you like I should have been. Before I knew it, you were a teenager who'd lost her mother, and you were looking to me for answers I didn't have. I felt helpless—like the situation was out of control—so I withdrew totally. I shouldn't have put off our time together—the chance to get to know the woman you've become." He looked at her, his eyes moist. "I wish now I'd paid more attention. I have a lot of regrets." He took her hand. "I'm sorry . . . but I want you to know I'm here for you now." He pulled her to her feet and stood in front of her, patting her shoulder. Then he put his arms around her and they shared another awkward hug. "I really hope you'll forgive me and give me a chance to be the kind of father I should have been all along."

Kristen nodded, the tears flowing freely down her face. "I've always wanted to be the kind of daughter you'd be proud of, Dad."

"You already are," he assured her. "Really, you are. I may not show it, but I've always cared about you, and I'm proud of you. I'll always be here for you."

"Thanks, Dad," she said, kissing him on the cheek. They sat down, and although Kristen still felt a little awkward, she knew this was the start od something fresh, and she was glad.

When Ryan walked up, he found Kristen smiling and sitting close to her father. He set the food down in front of them. "Is everything okay? Something's different."

"We were just talking about our family. I'm so anxious to see Brandon or to at least get some word about what is happening." Kristen sat up, not taking her eyes off Ryan. She felt happier than she had in a long time. The only thing that could make this better would be to have Brandon here with her.

Ryan looked like he wanted to ask something else, but they all turned when they heard footsteps coming down the hall. Their anxious eyes met Colonel Palmer's gaze as he entered the room.

He didn't mince words. "We've found the place where they're being held. The rescue team was attacked, and it's chaos. We need to dispatch a medical chopper for a downed officer. It's not clear who it is, so you need to be prepared in case it's your son. I'll let you know any other news as it comes in," he said, then, saluting, he walked away.

Kristen slumped against the seat, closing her eyes to stop from imagining the unimaginable. "What if it's Brandon?"

"Don't borrow trouble," Ryan cautioned, sitting beside her and taking her hand in his own. "Let's just wait and see."

She nodded and changed the subject. "You know, Brandon's letters had seemed more settled lately," she told Ryan. "I was really sorry I didn't get to see him before he was deployed." She turned to her father, who had gotten up to stand when the colonel had come in and now leaned against the door frame for support. "How did he seem to you before he left?"

"I did notice how happy he seemed. That's what mattered to me." He pushed himself up from the doorway, and Kristen went to him. She stood near him with folded arms until he tugged one of her hands free. Watching her, he slowly said, "I want both of my children to be happy. I always have." He patted her shoulder, then started through the door. "I'm going to see if I can find out what's going on."

Kristen smiled weakly, then slowly walked back to Ryan and sank down into her chair. She leaned over to put her head in her hands.

"So much is happening so fast. You, my father, Brandon. I feel like I'm on overload—but in a good way, sort of. It's hard to describe," she said with a little laugh.

"Yeah, me too. I never thought I'd see you and your father act this way." Ryan pulled her hands away from her face. "And as for us, I'm glad you came back into my life. We've wasted a lot of time." He smiled, and the dimple in his cheek deepened. "I wonder what Brandon will say."

"We'll find out soon," the general said, reentering the room. "The chopper is on its way."

CHAPTER 17

Rachel felt her stomach drop as she realized that Mofak Jassem stood in front of them. Her blood ran chill. She heard Brandon's rifle clatter to the ground when Mofak raised his gun as if to shoot her. At Brandon's apparent surrender, Mofak lowered his weapon and moved forward to retrieve the rifle, but Rachel saw her chance and took it, hitting his arm with all the force she could muster. As if Brandon had read her thoughts, he rushed by her and tackled Mofak. The men fell to the floor, each getting in several good punches as they grappled for Mofak's gun. Rachel felt like she was watching everything in slow motion. She knew she had to help Brandon, but it was as if she were rooted to the floor. She watched Mofak land a bone-crunching right hook, and as Brandon shook his head to recover, Mofak crawled toward the gun. At last, Rachel was able to make her feet obey her. She ran forward to grab the gun, but she was too late.

Just before she reached it, she heard the gun go off, and a blinding pain filled her arm. She instinctively grabbed the spot with her hand. Mofak stood there smiling at her, and she saw Brandon's eyes widen as she slumped against the wall. "Rachel," he breathed.

Mofak turned at Brandon's voice, and Brandon let out a warrior yell before punching Mofak with such fury that the man fell backward and slid across the floor. He landed in front of Rachel, and Brandon quickly took the gun that had fallen from Mofak's hands as he fell. Brandon pointed the gun at Mofak's head, his hands shaking with rage as Mofak glared up at him from the floor.

"Go ahead. Kill me," he taunted. "Make me a martyr for my cause." He looked over at Rachel. "Even now the blood is seeping out of her, and she will soon go into shock. You must act quickly."

Brandon looked at the man on the floor. He couldn't take his eyes off Mofak. He wiped the blood away from his nose and prepared to pull the trigger as anger welled up inside him. Just then the door burst open and several marines poured through, rushing toward them. Brandon turned the gun away from Mofak and took a deep breath. "I'm not going to kill you. That would be too easy. You're going to have to live with yourself," Brandon said, the anger in his eyes fading as he handed the gun to the soldiers. Brandon quickly went over to Rachel, who sagged against him.

"He shot me," she said, looking down at the blood seeping from her arm.

Brandon gently pulled her to the ground with him. "Try to be still and let me look at it."

"Are you okay, sir?" a marine asked as they watched three men haul Mofak away.

"I'm Dr. Shepherd. This is Dr. Fielding," he said, nodding to Rachel as he ripped the newly made hole in the black abayah fabric to reveal more of her arm. "We've been held captive here."

"I know, sir. We've been searching for you everywhere. It's a miracle we found you." The soldier put his gun aside and knelt down in front of Rachel. "Is her wound serious?"

It was almost impossible to examine Rachel with all the smoke, so Brandon simply continued to apply pressure. "We need to get her back to the base immediately," he pronounced, watching Rachel, who had turned very pale.

A soldier helped Rachel up, keeping both her and Brandon behind him as he moved toward the door, ready to defend them at any sign of trouble. He handed them off to a group of soldiers who waited down the hallway. Both Rachel and Brandon walked gingerly because of the wounds in their feet, but before they knew it they were outside, being greeted with pats on the back and "welcome home" sentiments from everyone they passed before getting into the back of a Humvee under heavy guard. A soldier handed them some bandages and antibiotics to treat their feet, which they gratefully accepted, but Rachel refused to let Brandon clean her gunshot wound. "It's fine," she told him. "I bandaged it myself."

He sighed at her stubbornness, but let her have her way. He looked at the concerned faces of those around him and knew that something more was up. "We're not out of the woods yet?" Brandon asked the soldiers.

"We didn't expect such fierce resistance," the soldier answered just as they heard the pop of more gunfire. "Sayed Fahim is in the house, and we're trying to capture him alive." He handed them some boots just as his radio crackled. He put it to his ear. "We've got wounded," he announced. He motioned for Brandon to follow him. "We need a doctor quick. The medics we have are overwhelmed with more wounded than we expected."

"I can help," Brandon reached back for Rachel, "but she's got a gunshot wound."

"A flesh wound," Rachel clarified, leaning forward. "And I can help, too."

Brandon smiled, once again impressed by her strength and dedication. "She comes with me then. We're a team."

"We're to keep you separate and safe, sir," the soldier answered, shaking his head. "That's protocol."

Brandon was adamant as he met the eyes of the soldier. "After what we've been through, we stay together."

The soldier shrugged in surrender. Brandon put his bandaged feet carefully into the boots, and he quickly laced them up. "Okay, follow me," the soldier said, pointing his gun downward and starting back toward the house.

Rachel had put her boots on while the men were talking, and she jumped out of the Humvee but didn't immediately follow them. Brandon looked back to see her taking off her abayah and crumpling it in her hands before throwing it back into the Humvee. "Welcome home," he called with a smile. She moved toward him, looking down appreciatively at her fatigues as she walked.

She smiled as she drew near to Brandon. "It feels so good to finally be free," she said, unable to contain the relief she felt at being able to wear her normal clothes.

Another explosion came from inside the house, and the soldier waved them on. "Hurry," he said. "We're bringing the wounded to the front of the convoy. A chopper is on its way. We need to move you up, but stay low."

Sand, combined with smoke, was making it difficult to breathe, but Rachel and Brandon quickly made their way to the front of the convoy. Two soldiers lay before them, one with a leg wound, the other with a gunshot wound in his hand. "I'll take the leg," Brandon announced and bent down to examine it. "Where's the medical kit?"

Rachel handed him the supplies, and he and Rachel worked side by side getting both soldiers bandaged and ready for transport. "You're a good team," one of the wounded soldiers commented. "You seem to know what the other needs before they even ask for it."

Brandon eyed Rachel, a smile playing around his lips. "Yes, we've had quite a bit of practice lately."

"Is it true you saved Sayed Fahim?" the soldier Brandon was treating asked. "You actually had his life in your hands and you saved him? I would have let that lowlife die."

Rachel's eyes radiated concern as she looked at Brandon. What could he say? He knew they would both get that question a lot now. Before he could answer, Rachel spoke up. "We're doctors," she said simply. "We took an oath."

Brandon looked at her with gratitude on his face. "We did what we had to do," was all he added before moving around to the other side of the Humvee, trying to get the wounded man ready to be loaded on the chopper.

The team leader walked toward them. "The area is secure," he announced. "We have several prisoners for transport."

"What about Sayed Fahim?" Brandon asked.

"He wasn't found," the team leader reported. "But we still have Mofak Jassem, and that's definitely something."

Brandon moved in closer to the building, wondering what had happened to Akmal. He was tempted to ask but didn't, not wanting to get into any explanations about what they'd been through just yet. The soldier clapped him on the shoulder. "The medevac should be here in five minutes."

Brandon turned around to find Rachel staring at him. She looked bone-tired as she pushed her hair back. "I bet you'd like a hot shower and some sleep," he said. Surprisingly, her eyes filled with tears, and she turned away from him.

Brandon came up to her and touched her uninjured arm. "What's wrong?" She could barely speak, and he knew her emotions had caught up with her. His own emotions were near the surface as well. He gently turned Rachel around and enfolded her in his arms, careful of her wound. Holding her to him, he whispered, "It's over. It's really over."

Laying her head on his chest, she tightened her arms around him. They stood there for several long moments, simply holding each other, until they heard the familiar whirring of the helicopter blades.

As the helicopter landed, they drew back, the shared look between them communicating the feelings they couldn't verbalize just yet. Blowing out a breath, they both immediately fell into a familiar routine, busying themselves with getting the wounded soldiers on board. When it came time for them to get inside, they stopped and gave one another a knowing look. Brandon saw in Rachel's gaze that she was remembering their last helicopter trip together as well. Finally Brandon stepped aboard and held out his hand for Rachel. "We're back where we started," he said.

She laughed and got in. "I don't think so," she told him, sitting on the seat in front of him. She reached back and lightly trailed her hand over his beard. "We'll never be the same," she said softly.

"I know," he answered, touching her cheek and grinning. "And you know what? I'm glad."

Sitting down, Brandon looked at the landscape around them, the home where they had been held and where they had found each other. They were alive, and they were free! It was an exultant feeling. The rotor blades picked up speed, and they were on their way back to base.

CHAPTER 18

Ryan, Kristen, and the general were all waiting with several soldiers near the helicopter's landing pad when it arrived. After the blades stopped spinning, Brandon exited first, stepping carefully and looking around as applause broke out. He smiled and waved before he reached back to help Rachel unload their patients. The other two medics that had been on board with the wounded followed them out as base personnel came to relieve them of the litters. It was then that he stopped and squinted, looking carefully at three figures near the front of the crowd. "Kristen! Dad!" he shouted as he started slowly jogging toward them. Kristen couldn't wait and ran into his arms as he enveloped her in a bear hug. "What are you doing here?"

"Saving you," she said, the tears rolling down her cheeks. "Did you think we wouldn't come?"

"Sir," Brandon said, putting Kristen down and acknowledging his father. "I'm sorry to bring you out all this way." He kept his arm around his sister, and she pulled her father into their embrace.

"Nonsense, boy," his father said, his smile turning to tears. "Of course we came. We had to make sure you were all right." The general pulled his son close, patting him enthusiastically on the back. "Glad to see you."

Kristen stepped back and watched them, her tears flowing freely as she looked around at several servicemen who were also discreetly wiping their faces. "Welcome home, Brandon," she said, squeezing him again.

"Well, hey, I came all the way to Iraq for you, *too,*" Ryan said as he stepped forward. "Do you have a hug for an old friend?"

Brandon shook his head. "I should have known you'd be here. You'll probably get some good press out of it."

Ryan pretended to look offended. "That would be your sister's area of expertise, not mine."

Ryan stuck out his hand, and Brandon took it as they pulled one another into a hug. "When did you guys get here?" Brandon asked.

"We haven't even been here a full day," Ryan said. "But your sister already had a secret meeting with a known terrorist group to secure your location and was almost part of a plot to raid the Security Summit."

Brandon looked back at Kristen, an astonished look on his face. "You did what?"

Kristen shook her head, clearly annoyed. "Don't listen to a word he says. You know how he goes on and on without making any sense." She glanced over at Colonel Palmer, who was dispersing the crowd.

"Yeah, I seem to remember that," Brandon said, laughing.

Ryan snorted. "Where's Alex when you need her? I'm outnumbered." They started toward the hospital doors, and Ryan noticed that Brandon was limping slightly. "Hey, were you wounded?"

Brandon grimaced. "Nothing I can't handle. But that reminds me. There's someone I want you to meet." He looked around for Rachel and saw that she had stopped near the helicopter and was sitting down on the ground with a medic. He immediately began walking toward them. "Wait right here for me, okay?"

He approached the chopper, his feet throbbing. "Hey, what's going on here?" he said as he reached them.

Rachel had her boot off and was wincing as the medic examined her foot, and the blood coming from her gunshot wound was hard to miss. "One of the concrete shards is embedded in my foot, and my gunshot wound is going to need a little more attention than I thought. I guess the adrenaline kept me from feeling much of it before," she explained, her expression wan.

Brandon hunched down and took over the exam. "Let me help. Why didn't you say something?" he asked Rachel as he cradled her heel.

"I told you, I didn't feel it before. I'm okay, Brandon. It's only superficial." She winced again and pulled her foot back a little, still favoring her left arm. "Don't touch it."

Brandon turned to the medic. "We better get her inside. We need lighting so we can get a better look at these wounds."

The medic nodded. "Shall I get a litter, sir?"

"No, I'll carry her," Brandon said. He went to scoop her up in his arms, but she held up her hands.

"Don't be ridiculous. You practically have the same wounds I do." She insisted on struggling to her feet, so he stayed by her side.

Her boot and sleeve were both soaked in blood, and the wound on her foot looked much worse than his. The shard was deeply embedded, and he knew they needed to get it out fast. She'd already lost a lot of blood from the gunshot wound, and by the look of her, she was going into shock. He needed to get her inside quickly.

"Brandon," she started, but her voice sounded far away. He caught her before she hit the ground.

He scooped her up and carried her toward the hospital doors. "We need a room."

The medic hurried to open the doors for him and secured a room. Brandon followed him and laid her on the bed before he began checking for any other wounds. There didn't seem to be any, so he concentrated on her feet and arm. He was shaking his head, trying to think clearly, as the door opened and Tyler Winthrop entered.

"What have we got here?" he asked Brandon.

"She has wounds to her feet, one serious, and a gunshot wound to her arm. It looked to be mostly a nick, but it was obviously worse than we thought. She's in shock," Brandon told him, trying to adjust the light so he could see Rachel's feet better. His hands were shaking, and though he tried to hide it, Tyler took notice.

"Brandon, why don't you let me take care of this? You can wait outside." Tyler bent over and began to examine her.

Brandon knew he would do Rachel no favors by insisting on treating her himself. He was exhausted, and he didn't want to take chances with her life. But he didn't want to leave her. "I'd like to stay with her, okay, Tyler?" He went around to the other side of her bed and took her hand. Her deathly white pallor scared him. He'd seen a lot as a doctor, but he'd never treated someone he cared about like this before. He took a deep breath.

Tyler came around to stand beside him. "From what I hear, you need to be checked yourself. When you get back, she'll probably be conscious and asking to see you." He gently pushed Brandon toward the door. "That's an order."

"Brandon?" Rachel called, her voice still weak.

He went to the edge of the bed. "I'm here." He grasped the hand of her good arm. "I'm not going anywhere."

She smiled. "I'm glad you're here."

Kissing the back of her hand, he brushed her hair back from her face. "Don't you be going anywhere yourself. I don't want to lose you now," he murmured under his breath. "Why didn't you tell me it was this bad?" he admonished.

Tyler didn't give Rachel a chance to answer as he came around the bed, a tray of instruments in his hand. "I'll take very good care of her, Brandon. Go get yourself checked out."

Rachel agreed. "I'll be here when you get back, I promise."

He chuckled. "I'm going to hold you to that. We have a dinner date, if I recall correctly."

She nodded and closed her eyes as Tyler started to administer anesthesia. "I'll be right back," he told her. Tyler nodded and kept working, deep in concentration. Brandon took one last look at Rachel, hesitant to part with her. They'd been through so much together. But one of the nurses came and escorted him to a triage area. Ryan, Kristen, and his father were there waiting.

"Is everything all right?" the general asked.

"The woman I was captured with is going into shock from her wounds. She was shot as we were trying to escape, but she's in good hands now. I also need to get my feet checked out. The guards took our boots, so when we were shot at during our escape, some pieces of concrete got embedded in our feet."

Kristen covered her hand with her mouth. "Are you going to be okay?"

Brandon waved his hand. "I'll be fine. I'm just worried about Rachel." The nurse came over and told Brandon they were ready for him. Brandon squeezed Kristen's arm when he saw her expression. "Don't worry about me, I'll be fine," he repeated, trying to reassure her. He walked down the hall to a treatment room, and the general followed him. As Brandon sat down on the bed and removed his boot, he looked up at his father. "Are you okay, sir?"

"Just worried about you, son." The general squeezed his hands together but didn't say anything for a moment. Finally, he spoke, his words measured, as if he'd thought long and hard about what he was going to say. "I was wondering if I'd ever have a chance to tell you some things in this life." He paused and seemed to be trying to control his emotions. "I wish I'd been a better father." Brandon started to interrupt him, but the general held up his hand. "I have a lot of regrets. After I was told you were missing in action, I really started to take a hard look at things." He came to Brandon and hugged him fiercely. "I love you, son. I'm so glad you're all right."

Brandon hugged his father back, the tears gathering in his own eyes. "I love you, Dad." Brandon patted his father's back. "I'm glad you're here."

The general wiped his eyes. "I've been a hardheaded fool," he said gruffly. "It took almost losing you to see that, and I don't plan on wasting any more time." He cleared his throat. "With you or your sister."

Brandon smiled. "Thanks, Dad. Really."

The general nodded. "Thank you, son, for being such a good example to your old man. Your mother would be so proud of you. You've never given up on anything you really wanted. If anyone could escape from terrorists, I knew it would be you." He straightened and looked at Brandon. "I'm proud of you, my boy."

The nurse came into the room and began setting up the area so she could clean Brandon's foot wounds. The general watched her for a moment, then moved next to Brandon. Clapping him on the back, he put his arm around him and squeezed. "I'll wait for you outside."

"Okay," Brandon said, wincing at the nurse's ministrations. "I shouldn't be long. But Dad, I had a lot of time to think, too, and when things settle down, I'd like to tell you about a few things I've learned—like where Mom is now and how we can be reunited with her for eternity."

His father's eyes widened, but then he smiled. "I'd like that, son."

Brandon watched his father leave, surprised at the turn of events. He couldn't wait to share this with Kristen—and Rachel.

* * *

Ryan and Kristen sat down. "It seems like all we've been doing is waiting." Kristen sighed.

"It's probably time to think about going home," Ryan answered. "Do you think Brandon will come with us? I bet they'd let him."

"Having seen the look on his face when he was speaking about Rachel, I doubt it," Kristen said ruefully. "I wish he would though."

They watched the general come out of the room where Brandon was being treated and stand outside as if he were going to stay there and wait. "I think things will be better between us as a family from now on," Kristen mused aloud.

Ryan put his arm around her. "I'm glad." It felt so right to be with him, like she just fit, and she leaned her head against him.

After an hour, Brandon emerged from the room and came toward them with both the general and the colonel flanking him. As the threesome approached the family, the colonel hung back, allowing them a bit of privacy. Brandon and the general both looked happy, and Kristen stood, wanting to be a part of everything. "How are you?" she asked.

Her father reported for him. "He's dehydrated and has some nasty cuts on his feet, but he insists he's fine. And he refuses to go to Germany and wants to stay here."

Brandon laughed. "They'll probably make me go to Germany anyway. I appreciate you guys coming—it means the world to me. But the colonel wants me in for debriefing ASAP, and that will last days. And I need to stay with Rachel for a while. My tour is up in two months, so I'll be home soon. But I want to talk a bit more before you fly home—I know Dad's made arrangements already—and I want you to meet Rachel. Oh, and I really want to talk to you, Kristen. You're glowing, and I want to know why."

She hugged him briefly. "I want to talk to you, too. A lot has happened. I think you'll be happy for me though." Ducking her head, she smiled and pulled a bag of Skittles out of her pocket. "There are some new flavors in there," she said, handing it to him.

Brandon shook his head and smiled. "You know, Skittles are what started this whole adventure. I'll tell you about it when you meet Rachel.

He beckoned everyone toward Rachel's room, lifting a brow when he saw Ryan take Kristen's hand. Ryan just grinned—happy to be caught.

"Thanks again," Brandon said, looking down at the Skittles as Colonel Palmer stepped forward.

"I'm sorry, Brandon, but there's still a lot to be done."

Brandon grimaced but smiled at his family before following the colonel out. "I'll see you soon. You can count on it."

CHAPTER 19

Kristen slowly walked back to her trailer from the showers. It felt heavenly to be clean and to wear a fresh outfit. She'd even left her hair down, although it was already picking up some blowing sand. The sky had begun to darken and looked ominous. She swung her little plastic bag of toiletries, smiling at the soldiers around her. Everyone seemed to be heading for the chow hall. She wondered if Ryan was already there. These last few days had been incredible—life changing, in fact. Her world had been turned upside down, and yet somehow, everything seemed right.

She felt the first raindrop and looked at the sky in surprise. Within moments, the sky was totally black and the rain was coming down in torrents. She was completely soaked, and her feet were getting sucked into the deep, sticky mud the sand had suddenly turned into. She tried to cover her head with her bag, but it didn't offer much protection. Finally reaching her trailer, she fumbled with the handle, trying to open it, but it wouldn't budge. "Come on!" she yelled in frustration.

A large hand covered hers. "Let me help you with that."

Kristen turned and saw Ryan standing next to her, water dripping down his face. "Thanks. I didn't think it rained in Iraq," she said. "It must be my luck."

He chuckled and cupped her face in his hand. "I would say that rain is a lucky thing for you. After all, the last rainstorm I remember brought you back into my life, still as spunky as ever."

"Spunky?" she said, raising her eyebrows. "In a good way, right?"

He bent down and kissed her, the rain softer and slower around them now. Then he leaned back to look at her. "It looks like it's letting up already. Which is good, because I think the handle to your trailer might be broken."

She laid her head on his chest. "Well, I think my feet are permanently entombed in this muck anyway. I can't move."

"All the better for me," he said, lifting her head to give her a playful grin. She laughed. "What would Brandon say?"

"What would Brandon say, indeed," Ryan murmured. "I think he's happy for us. He would probably tell us that himself if he could ever stop talking about his new faith or if we could tear him away from Rachel. They seem pretty close."

"I'm happy for him, and I like what he says about the idea of seeing my mother again and how important families are," she said. "He's waited so long to find someone to love. Rachel seems like a perfect match for him." She tried once more to lift her foot out of the mud and then gave up. "You know, they're both doctors, they've both served in Iraq, and they've both shared their experience in captivity. They have a lot in common. Unlike us. We're practically opposites—especially opposites politically—and we don't even live in the same town," she added, watching his reaction.

He was silent for a moment, looking at her as if he wanted to memorize her features. "I've been meaning to talk to you about your political views," he said finally. "And I know that Brandon had talked about wanting you to move closer to your father." He rubbed his hand over his chin. Then, as if thinking out loud, he said, "I definitely wouldn't mind you living in Boston again, but I'd want you to be happy. I bet we could work something out so that no matter where we were or what election was being held—or whose side we were on politically—we could be together. It would just take a little trust."

She touched her hand to his cheek. "I trust you, Ryan. Completely. Any reserve I had you've broken down, and I would hope that I've done the same for you. I promise I'll always be worthy of your trust. You can count on that." As she watched the emotions flit across his face, she knew she had earned that trust, and it made her feel almost giddy with happiness. She couldn't keep the smile from her face. "Ever since Brandon's return, everything just seems, I don't know, different somehow—in a good way. I feel completely peaceful and happy—in Iraq of all places."

He grinned at her, his hair wet with rain and beginning to curl—that boyish Ryan again.

He pushed her hair back from her face, wiping the rain from her cheeks with his thumbs. Then he searched her expression for a moment. "I want you to know how much I love you. I think I've always loved you, Kristy, and I know I always will," he finished and then bent to touch his lips to hers.

Kristen closed her eyes and wrapped her arms around his neck. She didn't have to say that she'd always loved him. They both knew it. Today, all *was* fair, at least in love.

About the Author

Julie and her husband, Brian, are the parents of six children, and her greatest joy is being a mother. She graduated from Brigham Young University with a degree in Secondary Education—English teaching, and she currently teaches a journalism course for BYU Continuing Education. She enjoys traveling (especially to her home country of Canada), trying new things, reading, writing, and spending time with her family. She has a large collection of books, and when she's not busy being a mom, teaching, or writing, you will more than likely find her browsing through bookstores to add to that collection or reading the treasures she's found.